The Maid

YASUTAKA TSUTSUI

Translated by Adam Kabat

ALMA BOOKS

ALMA BOOKS LTD
London House
243–253 Lower Mortlake Road
Richmond
Surrey TW9 2LL
United Kingdom
www.almabooks.com

First published by Alma Books Ltd in 2010
Kazoku Hakkei (The Maid) by Yasutaka Tsutsui
Copyright © 1972 Yasutaka Tsutsui
Original Japanese edition published by Shinchosha Publishing Co., Ltd.
English translation rights arranged with Yasutaka Tsutsui through Andrew
Nurnberg Associates Ltd. / Japan Foreign-Rights Centre.
English translation © 1990 Kodansha International Ltd
All rights reserved.

Reprinted 2011

This is a work of fiction. Names, characters, places and incidents either
are the product of the author's imagination or are used fictitiously, and any
resemblance to actual persons, living or dead, business establishments, events
or locales is entirely coincidental.

Printed in Great Britain by CPI Antony Rowe

ISBN: 978-1-84688-099-5

CONTENTS

THE MAID

1

The Plain of Emptiness

Red flowers were blooming in the front yard, but Nanase had no idea what they were: the names of the flowers did not interest her.

The Ogata residence was a bright, middle-class home with a large veranda. Nanase rang the doorbell, then waited on the porch. The neighbourhood was silent except for the distant whistles of suburban trains.

Sakiko Ogata opened the door. She was in her forties but her drab kimono made her seem much older.

"Please come in."

Nanase introduced herself, and Sakiko seemed to relax, smiling as she showed her into the living room. Nanase noted that every piece of furniture was new. Apparently it was a policy of the household to redecorate the house constantly with cheap new furnishings.

After reading Nanase's reference, Sakiko looked up at the girl and smiled again. "Mrs Akiyama writes very highly of you."

Nanase nodded slightly. She knew what the reference said without having to read it.

When Nanase applied for a new job, the mistress of the household would usually enquire into why Nanase had left her former workplace, trying to determine indirectly whether she had gone of her own free will or if she had been dismissed. Although Nanase had expected the same from Sakiko, Sakiko didn't ask a thing.

Nor did Sakiko show the house to the new maid, another common practice. She simply sat facing her, looking bored and distracted.

Nanase read Sakiko's mind. But all she could find were odds and ends of consciousness.

The bathroom tiles are starting to chip. For tonight's dinner, I'll make stir-fried beef and green peppers with a miso sauce. There are problems with the TV's vertical tuning, and the lock on the shed is broken. I'll have to tell Nanase that the rice cooker isn't working, but the store will be delivering a new one tomorrow.

Sakiko's thoughts did not extend beyond such household matters. It was debatable whether these could even be called thoughts. They were simply insignificant notions tumbling about on the plain of an empty consciousness.

Was Sakiko running away from something? Nanase had encountered this type of consciousness any number of times. It was especially common among weak, middle-aged, middle-class women who were used to being ignored and who – even while fully aware that they were despised – blocked it out of their minds.

Sakiko glanced at Nanase's suitcase, thought about how heavy it looked, imagined how tired she must be after lugging it up the hill, and then finally hit upon the idea of offering her tea.

"Let's have a cup of tea in the kitchen," she said.

Sakiko stood up and smiled once more at Nanase. Her smile was without meaning. But what surprised Nanase was that there wasn't even an *unconscious* expression of warmth.

Nanase could not recall when she first realized she had the power to read people's minds. But not once during her eighteen years had she ever thought that it was a particularly unusual ability. She even felt that there must be a lot of people with this power, her logic being that anyone who could do this would keep it secret, as she herself had done.

For her, mind-reading was neither a plus nor a minus. She thought of it as another sense, like hearing or sight. It differed slightly from the other senses only in that it required a bit of effort to use. Nanase referred to this as "unlatching", setting it apart from other mental functions. And she was very careful to keep this "latch" fastened when she wasn't using it. She had learnt from this experience that if she left the latch open, other people's thoughts would come flooding in non-stop, leaving her unable to distinguish between what was spoken and what was thought – an extremely dangerous situation in which she might inadvertently reveal her powers.

That day, as Sakiko was explaining various things to her, Nanase occasionally undid the latch and peered into Sakiko's mind. But each time, all she saw was careworn everyday concerns strewn over a barren wasteland. She couldn't even make out what feelings Sakiko had towards the members of her family.

Hisakuni Ogata, the head of the household, managed the general-affairs division of a shipbuilding company. There were two children: Eiko, who was a senior at a women's university, and Junichi, who had just started college this year. Eiko was beautiful; Junichi was pale and slender. Both inherited their father's hedonistic tendencies. That was about all Nanase was able to learn from Sakiko. And most of this came from Sakiko's own lips.

The day drew to a close, but neither Hisakuni nor the children returned home. This seemed to be a common occurrence, as Sakiko was unperturbed.

After a simple dinner, Sakiko made no more attempts at conversing with Nanase. She simply looked absently at the living-room TV. She wasn't watching it, merely staring at it.

Hisakuni returned shortly after eleven.

Nanase was tired, but she'd stayed awake so she could introduce herself to her new employer.

"Are the children back yet?" Hisakuni asked his wife as he entered the living room. Nanase tried to greet him, but he ignored her presence.

"No, not yet," replied Sakiko, who introduced Nanase with her usual smile.

"How do you do." Nanase bowed and undid the latch.

Hisakuni gave Nanase a quick glance, and greeted her with a perfunctory nod, all the time comparing her to the bevy of nightclub hostesses whose company he'd just been enjoying. He seemed to have powers of observation befitting his position as a general-affairs manager.

"Would you like something to drink?" asked Sakiko.

Hisakuni looked at the wall clock. "A cup of tea."

He didn't want any tea. He was concerned about Eiko, although he would never admit this, even to himself. He had convinced himself that he had long ago given up on his delinquent daughter, but he had stopped thinking about her only on the surface of his consciousness. Once he heard her excuse for coming home late, he could set his mind at rest. He knew that it would be a lie, but he still wanted to hear it.

Nanase realized this had nothing to do with paternal affection. It was jealousy.

Hisakuni thought of his wife as a domestic animal, hardly worthy of his attention. Almost ten years had passed since he last had sexual relations with her, which he'd only managed to do by recalling her youthful beauty. Now he didn't even talk to her. Anything said out of pity would only make him despise her, which Sakiko also sensed. As her attitude frequently made clear to him, she preferred to be ignored rather than despised.

The only things that really mattered to Hisakuni were his job and young women. And even his feelings about girls were grossly exaggerated as a way to arouse himself. All Nanase could see in his mind was emptiness.

"So you're eighteen?" he asked, before realizing he had spoken in the exact tone he'd used with club hostesses. "It's great to be young," he added hastily. "Great to be young."

Hisakuni was sleeping with a nightclub hostess who wasn't much older than Nanase. Setsuko was her name. She had quite a figure.

"How true," responded Sakiko automatically, her eyes glued to the late-night TV show.

Eiko came home drunk. A boyfriend had plied her with liquor, taken her to a motel, and then driven her home.

She took one look at Nanase and thought that with the maid here she could get by without giving an excuse for coming home late. Then she reconsidered and decided to offer some brief explanation.

"Yoshie didn't come tonight. She could've given me a lift so I could have got back earlier. But I had to wait for Kitani to take me home. Even though he seemed to want to dance more, he went out of his way to drive me back."

"That's nice." Hisakuni smiled and nodded.

"Kitani's so good-natured," Sakiko added.

"I want some tea," demanded Eiko, who then started making small talk with Nanase. "Your name is

Nanase? Can I call you Nana then? You're eighteen? You're so lucky. I wish I could be eighteen again."

Eiko made no attempt to get the tea herself. Both she and her father seemed to think it was perfectly natural to have Sakiko make it for her. Sakiko herself didn't mind taking orders from her daughter. Eiko detested Sakiko for her insipidness.

While she was talking, Eiko was replaying, almost physically, the sexual scene she had just experienced with Kitani. By means of this "aftertaste", she could indulge in her lust even while exchanging pleasantries. For Nanase, who still had no experience with men, the action going on inside Eiko's head was extremely interesting.

As she chattered on, Eiko's excitement grew. Throwing caution to the wind, she started talking openly about her male friends.

"...at which point Kitani deliberately stepped on Takada's foot. Then Takada stopped giving me strange looks."

Eiko's playfulness was gradually making Hisakuni suspicious. He was now convinced that his daughter had just come back from some immoral goings-on. She's trying to pull the wool over my eyes, he thought, as he imagined Eiko and the college student Kitani, whom he had met only once, frolicking stark naked.

Hisakuni's version of Eiko's events was extremely graphic. Nanase peered deeper into his mind.

11

Hisakuni had superimposed the naked image of his daughter over that of the hostess Setsuko – not to suppress his anger, rather to excite himself. As his daughter chattered away, he continued smiling at her cheerfully.

Eiko had noticed, with a girl's intuition, that whenever she talked about her boyfriends, her father's smile took on a hint of lewdness. She despised her father for trying to fan his passions through her. And she hated the crass way he entertained clients at expensive clubs every night so he could drink and party without having to pay for it. However, she had no idea that her father was sleeping with a hostess provided by one of his subcontractors.

It surprised Nanase a bit that in spite of the arrival of herself, a stranger, this evening, the behaviour of the family seemed to be no different from what it might be usually. Perhaps this was because the members of this family were strangers to one another. She doubted that the presence of the son, Junichi, would change the atmosphere much.

The late show ended, and Junichi still hadn't returned. The family seemed unconcerned. No one gave him a thought.

"Time for bed." Once the TV set was turned off, Hisakuni stood up.

It dawned upon Nanase that this semblance of family harmony had been precariously maintained by the background noise coming from the television.

Once it had been turned off, the family was assailed by a suffocating silence. There was nothing left to do but go to bed.

Hisakuni stopped suddenly just as he was leaving the living room. He had overlooked the fact that his daughter had come home late. Should he say something to her? He told himself that it was a parent's duty to make some comment, if only for the sake of form. At the least, he had to play his role of loving father in this drama of family harmony.

"From now on, I'd like you to get home at a decent hour," he said in as light a tone as possible. His voice sounded forced.

"I'm sorry."

Eiko apologized right away, having anticipated Hisakuni's comment from the moment he stopped in his tracks. But, of course, she couldn't let it go at that. She had to play *her* role of the mischievous daughter. And she had to retaliate.

"But I never imagined that you'd get home before me on a Saturday night." She laughed.

Hisakuni also laughed. He was embarrassed.

And Sakiko twisted her face and came out with her version of a laugh.

Nanase, who felt quite unable to laugh, pretended to be tidying up. This family laughter did nothing for the tension; all it did was underline the emptiness.

Even after everyone had gone to bed, Junichi had yet to return home.

13

Nanase had been provided with a small room off the entrance hall. The occasional roar of cars speeding down the road outside kept waking her up. At dawn, around four thirty or five, she heard the resilient sound of a sports car disappearing into the adjoining garage. Junichi had his own key, so Nanase didn't bother to get up.

On Sunday morning, the whole family slept in. Sakiko finally woke up just before ten. Now that Nanase was here, she seemed to be deliberately taking it easy.

Around noon, when Nanase passed by Junichi's room, she could hear mumbling. Not knowing what it was, she stopped to listen. Eiko, who had just got up, giggled.

"He's talking in his sleep. It surprises everyone at first."

Junichi woke up just before two and asked for a huge bowl of miso soup, claiming it was good for hangovers. The previous night he had downed half a bottle of whisky at a girl's apartment. She had been Junichi's classmate in junior high school. Now she worked as a club hostess. Setsuko was her name. She had quite a figure.

Father and son were sleeping with the same woman! What's more, Junichi was aware of this. Nanase stared at Junichi. While drinking in bed with Setsuko, he would bad-mouth his father as a way of releasing his hostility.

"Is there something strange about my face?"

All at once Junichi plunked down his bowl on the kitchen table and looked up at Nanase. Taking advantage of the fact that they were alone, he had hoped to embarrass her. Nanase looked away, acting embarrassed.

"No, no... nothing special..."

Junichi, the narcissist, enjoyed making girls uncomfortable.

That day Nanase kept her latch fastened until supper. She had been extremely disturbed to discover Setsuko in Junichi's thoughts. Nanase had been actively reading people's minds for ten years or so, and there was very little that surprised her any more, but this time she had definitely received a jolt.

How horrible, she thought. I've never met such a horrible family before.

It was an unspoken rule that every Sunday the whole family would stay home. This was the day when the Ogatas, to avoid a complete break-up, would show just how family-minded they really were.

The sun was shining.

Hisakuni spent the whole time pottering about the garden. The rest of the family were watching television or holed up in their rooms. Sometimes they'd wander about the house aimlessly and, whenever they ran into each other, they'd exchange empty jokes, laugh together or make innocuous wisecracks at Hisakuni in the garden.

15

"Sis, you've put weight back on your behind."

"Did you have a good time last night? Ha-ha."

"Mum, you're stooping."

"Oh Dad, you have such awful taste in sweaters."

"Father, you should take off your cap. Tomorrow at work, everyone will think you got a tan while playing golf."

"Don't be ridiculous. The underlings who escort clients around get golf tans. I'm far too important."

"Junichi, you're getting a pot belly."

"Mum, you have a grey hair. Let me pull it out – look."

Sakiko was the only one who never answered back no matter what. She simply responded with her usual smile.

Everyone in the family knew their roles. They'd roam through the house with malice in their hearts, avoiding physical contact at any cost, and adopting poses they had mastered out of soap operas.

Nanase found it suffocating. The previous night she predicted that she wouldn't last here very long.

At exactly seven o'clock, when dinner was ready and the evening news began, the whole family assembled in the living room. This was another custom of the Ogata household, although no one said it out loud. If they had, the custom would have instantly vanished.

"Would you like a whisky?" Sakiko asked her husband.

There's not much sake left. I hope he'll want whisky.

"I'll have a little sake."

They don't have sake at the club.

Of course. He can't drink sake at his club. Humph, what an old fogey. I'll show him.

"Give me a whisky," said Junichi. Then, afraid he had sounded antagonistic, he quickly added, "I have to get up early tomorrow, so I need a drink to put me to sleep."

"That's one way to cure a hangover," Eiko taunted. The fact that she and her brother had exactly the same metabolism, even though their gender was different, sent shivers down Eiko's spine.

Junichi laughed, but made no reply. In the first place, he thought his sister was an idiot like her mother before her. But what he really couldn't forgive was her refusal, unlike her mother, to recognize her own stupidity. Incredibly enough, she even believed that she was some sort of intellectual.

What a hopeless case.

Even more upsetting was the fact that she was pilfering their father's savings to spend on clothes. *What right does she have to anything when she'll only end up getting married?* But Eiko would maintain that she was the kind of woman who required a lot of money to show off her good looks.

The affected bitch!

"Nana, could you get the whisky and sake?" asked Sakiko.

Nanase went to the kitchen, where she deliberated for a while over which vessel to heat the sake in and which glass to use. Of course, by reading Sakiko's mind, she already knew the answer. Sakiko thought only of such details.

However, for Nanase, this was dangerous. If she did exactly as Sakiko wished, her uncanny intuition might arouse suspicion. In such instances, Nanase would consciously play the fool.

When Nanase brought the wrong glasses on purpose, Eiko corrected her ever so gently.

"Oh, aren't there smaller whisky glasses? Those are champagne glasses."

Moron! Bumpkin!

Eiko felt nothing but contempt for all other women.

"It doesn't matter. I prefer the bigger ones," said Junichi.

Don't be a smart-arse, Eiko, you interfering bitch!

Eiko grinned.

Humph. You think you're so hot. You lush!

Hisakuni also grinned. "You seem to have a soft spot for Nana."

Is that the only thing you're interested in? Dirty old man.

"I have a soft spot for all girls."

Including your mistress, you senile bastard.

"Is that so?" Hisakuni had no other answer.

Hisakuni feared youth more than was warranted. He had learnt from painful experience that problems at work often arose when young employees defied their superiors – with a terrible obstinacy. If Junichi should ever rebel, he could imagine only too well how his own weakness and confusion would put a quick end to any parental authority. This insecurity made him quiver with fear.

But Nanase's observations of Junichi told her that Hisakuni was vastly overestimating him. Even if Junichi defied his father, he himself was so insecure he'd give in with the first counterattack. One roar would strike terror in his heart.

Fear and guilt lay behind the hatred and contempt he felt for his father. Junichi himself didn't realize this, but it would take only the smallest incident to make these feelings erupt.

"Junichi, you can't sweet-talk Nana. She already heard you talking in your sleep," said Eiko.

"Oh, I'm in for it now!"

Junichi adopted a comic pose and let out a shriek. Then he stared at Nanase with upturned eyes, and asked in a mock nervous tone, "So what did I say?"

I can't take it any more, thought Nanase. A family that argues all the time would be a vast improvement over this. Suddenly she was overcome with an urge to destroy their precarious outward harmony.

"You called out a woman's name," she said with a giggle.

Junichi stopped eating.

Eiko smiled to herself and licked her lips in anticipation.

"A woman's name?" asked Hisakuni in a slightly louder voice as he smiled at Nanase. In order to uphold his hegemonic position as head of the family, he felt obliged to speak out even in matters of little importance. "What name?"

Nanase answered immediately, without batting an eyelash. "He said 'Setsuko'."

For a moment Hisakuni's face turned red.

Junichi's body tensed.

It's finally happened... Shit! The talkative bitch!

Eiko picked up on the quick change in the moods of her father and brother, and sensed something was up.

But that's strange. I heard him talking in his sleep too, and I'm sure he didn't mention any woman's name.

I've blown it, thought Nanase. She hadn't realized that Eiko had also overheard him. Now she'd have to divert Eiko's thoughts to the confrontation between father and brother. In order to do so, she'd have to provoke their hostility and suspicions even more.

"And then..." Nanase acted as if she were lost in thought. She was searching for the name of Setsuko's club, but she could not find it. Junichi's thoughts were centred on his father's expression and demeanour; Hisakuni was going over the possibility that the Setsuko he knew might also know his son.

"And then?" asked Hisakuni. "Did he say something else?"

"Oh, come on," Junichi quickly joked. "Give me a break, Nana."

This said, any further incitement by Nanase would be risky, for it would draw everyone's attention to her. Nanase abandoned her plan to reveal the name of the club. In this way, an irreparable break-up was avoided.

For a while a tense silence continued.

Hisakuni burst out laughing.

"Is that so? Setsuko? Ha-ha-ha."

Having overcome his resistance to saying the name out loud, his spirits rose.

Once more the whole family broke into hollow laughter.

Balance was restored.

There are lots of girls with the name Setsuko.

Something's up. I'm sure of it. I wonder who Setsuko is.

The maid talks too much. I'll have to do something about that.

In contrast to their various dark thoughts, the topic of conversation turned to television. The family jabbered away with a wholesome animation right out of a situation comedy.

Nanase sensed trouble. Junichi seemed to be planning something.

As she expected, Junichi's plot against her gradually took shape and was put into action two days later. He lifted from his parents' wallets just enough money to be missed, and then confided in his mother that he had seen Nanase stealing the money.

21

Nanase knew all about it beforehand, but was helpless to do anything. If she had launched a counterattack, there was the danger that her power would be revealed to Junichi.

Strangely enough, Sakiko didn't say anything to Hisakuni. It occurred to Nanase that Sakiko might have thought that there was nothing so odd about a maid pilfering a bit of money, and she wasn't going to bother over it. From time to time, she'd undo her latch and read Sakiko's mind.

It was still a junkyard of everyday matters. Although Nanase couldn't find the incident of "Nana's kleptomania", it was surely bumping around somewhere among the flotsam and jetsam. Oddly enough, no distinction was made between the important and the unimportant; everything lay scattered about evenly.

From Sakiko's attitude, Nanase guessed that she might not be fired after all, but this prediction proved wrong. In fact, all the while Sakiko had been mulling over Nanase's next place of employment. She realized this when Sakiko broached the subject.

"The name of the family is Jimba," said Sakiko. "The children are getting bigger now, but they still need looking after. There're thirteen in the family, so you'll have your work cut out for you. It's a shame to let you go, but if you don't mind, I'd like to send you over there."

"Thirteen?" Inwardly Nanase breathed a sigh of relief.

"But they're good people – a nice family. And you'll get a better salary."

Nanase read Sakiko's mind, but all she could find were samples of roundabout expressions that wouldn't hurt the girl's feelings. However, it was clear to Nanase that she was no longer wanted, so she gave her consent.

"I'll take you up on the offer."

Sakiko nodded. "We'll miss you." She was, of course, without emotion.

Just what kind of mental make-up does this woman have, Nanase wondered. Her emotions, the workings of her mind, were completely indecipherable, as if she were hiding her true feelings. When she thought this far, Nanase had a sudden shock.

What if she *were* hiding her true feelings?

In order to do this, wasn't she deliberately strewing these ordinary matters over the surface of her consciousness? The same way countless fragments of aluminium scattered throughout the sky would block a radar screen and confuse the enemy?

Of course. This would explain why Nanase had been unable to find in Sakiko's thoughts any hint she was looking for a new job for her.

Which meant that Sakiko was aware of Nanase's telepathic powers.

If that were the case, then Sakiko herself was telepathic.

Who would have dreamt such a thing?

Sakiko was the one she should have been most cautious of. And yet, up until now, Nanase had made light of her for her weak spirit and, like the rest of the family, had completely ignored her.

Was she really telepathic? Or was she simply trying to hide her remarkable intuitive powers? Or was it telepathy after all?

If so, answer in your mind.

If so, answer in your mind.

Nanase stared at Sakiko as she repeatedly called out to her inwardly.

However, Sakiko was without expression. And the barren images spreading over the landscape of her consciousness remained the same as always.

Nanase felt a cold shiver go down her spine.

Was this how a telepathic wife would have to act to protect the outward peace and harmony of her family? Was this the only behaviour possible? And if Sakiko represented the declining years of a woman with telepathy, then would Nanase too end up like this someday? No, no, it wasn't just a matter of telepathy. Wouldn't any woman with a highly developed intuition have to hide her ability and, in order to maintain even a semblance of family harmony, have to pretend to possess the kind of mental make-up that is despised and ignored? And ironically wouldn't she then be considered the epitome of a good wife?

Hisakuni wrote Nanase's reference.

When he handed it to her, Nanase read Hisakuni's mind and was relieved to find that there was nothing in the letter that would be particularly damaging.

Which meant that, in the end as well, Sakiko had said nothing to Hisakuni about Nanase's theft. This might have been because Sakiko knew that Junichi was the real thief.

But Nanase didn't care any more. The following day, shortly after noon, she left the Ogata residence. She had been there exactly one week.

Go ahead and continue your play-acting as long as you like – go on with this family circus for ever, thought Nanase. She passed through the gate, not even bothering to look back at the house, as tidy as a stage set.

In the yard, the red flowers were still blooming profusely.

2

Prisoners
of Dirt

The Jimbas ran a large shoe store on an avenue close to a suburban railway junction. The building extended all the way to the street behind, and the family lived in the back. Husband and wife took turns running the shop.

As soon as Nanase arrived at the Jimbas', she noticed a strange smell emanating from the whole house – the dark rooms in the rear, the living room, the kitchen, even the maid's room – and enveloping the entire family.

Every household has its own smell. Sometimes only the people who live there can perceive it; in other cases the reverse is true. Often the smell does not really exist but is only a psychologically induced association. However, nothing in any of the homes Nanase had worked in compared with the intensity of this odour. Needless to say, the smell wasn't at all like the fragrance of the row of cedar and cypress clogs in the store.

Even stranger was the fact that no one in the family seemed to notice the stench.

"What's that smell, I wonder?"

Nanase let this slip while she was being interviewed by Koichiro, the head of the Jimba household. But Koichiro simply raised his chin ever so slightly and wriggled his nose.

"Hmm… Maybe something's burning in the kitchen."

Although Koichiro had just turned fifty, he already seemed worn out, but he was a good-natured, plain-spoken man. Nanase knew that candour and gentleness in a middle-aged man existed often only on the surface, but as far as she could tell by probing Koichiro's mind, they seemed to be the real thing. Basically he lacked the craftiness of most shopkeepers. He never asked Nanase why she had left her last job; in fact, he had not thought to make such an enquiry. This seemed to be his first experience hiring someone. Nanase liked him.

"My old lady's worked herself to the bone," said Koichiro as he scratched his head in embarrassment. He was totally without affectation. "She still insists on doing the kitchen work, even though the doctor told her not to. But you see, we have eleven children."

"Yes, I heard from Mrs Ogata."

"Oh, is that so?" Koichiro seemed surprised. He stared blankly at Nanase.

Even while they were talking, the little girls Yoko and Etsuko were running up and down the hallway, and sometimes Koichiro would have to disappear into the store to serve a customer. In this family, chaos had become commonplace, but for some reason a strange kind of order reigned. It occurred to Nanase that this might be the result of the odour pervading the house.

After she relaxed a bit in her tiny room, the wife, Kaneko, came to see her.

"It's not going to be a piece of cake here. Prepare yourself for the worst," Kaneko said, laughing.

By reading her mind, Nanase could tell that Kaneko was determined to take it easy. Still, Nanase was not afraid of hard work; even the image in Kaneko's consciousness of the heap of washing piled up in the laundry room did not faze her.

"Shinichi, my eldest son, graduated from college this year and is working for a shipbuilding company. His brother, Akio, is in college... uh, what year is he, I wonder? My eldest girl, Michiko, is in high school. She's studying for her entrance exams for junior college, so she doesn't help with the housework. Next comes, uh... my third boy, Keisuke, who's in high school. Oh, I'm sorry – Keisuke's my fourth son, in junior high. Ryuzo's my third son. Then..."

Kaneko, who was rather obese, chatted with a sort of sloppy animation, displaying a mouth full of gold teeth.

Of course, Kaneko had become a pig. What she had gone through raising all these children, plus having resigned herself to the task for the years to come, had formed such a thick sediment in her consciousness that it blocked everything else out. Nanase sighed.

While she was talking to Kaneko, the stench kept getting stronger. It was so sharp Nanase began to wonder whether it was coming from the maid's room.

"What was this room up until now?" Nanase suddenly asked.

"Huh?"

For a moment Kaneko couldn't understand the question; then, before Kaneko spoke, the answer appeared as an image in her mind. The room had been used for storage.

"I must be your first live-in maid."

Nanase had jumped the gun, speaking before Kaneko had a chance to answer. Nanase immediately caught her mistake, for Kaneko was staring at her suspiciously.

I wonder how she knew that?

Nanase cursed herself.

Oh, I did it again!

In all likelihood there was no one who knew that Nanase had this ability to read people's minds.

When she was a child, she hadn't thought of her power as anything special. As a result, she would often get into trouble for reading the thoughts of adults around her and laughing at them. In time she began to learn instinctively to hide her ability, and eventually she learnt how to control her power by deliberately shutting out people's streams of consciousness. Now she realized only too well how the exposure of her telepathy would spell her own doom. Even so, when she first met someone, there were times when it was necessary to keep the "latch" of her mind open, making her unable to distinguish between what was spoken and what was thought. At such times, she would often inadvertently expose her power. Fortunately, most people, like Kaneko, were unable to conceive of the likes of a telepathist, and were never very suspicious. So Nanase was less in danger of being found out than she feared.

All the same, you can never be too careful, Nanase would warn herself repeatedly. Get caught once and the game is up.

"I know you've just arrived but…" said Kaneko hesitantly. "I wonder if you'd do the laundry. I have to go shopping for dinner."

Since I'm paying her a much higher salary than usual, she'll have to work that much harder.

Of course, any housewife would think the same, so Nanase wasn't particularly put out. She nodded and stood up.

As Kaneko led her to the laundry room next to the bath, Nanase stole a glance into the dining area. Three used rice bowls had been left sitting on the table.

As soon as Nanase had opened the glass doors and entered the large room with its pile of laundry exactly as she'd seen in Kaneko's mind, the ever-present stench got even stronger. Nanase recoiled, overcome by a wave of nausea.

Nanase wondered if this was the source of the odour. All of the underclothes were soiled black; the male garments were particularly dirty and smelly, and the socks were the worst. Nanase felt sick. However, while Kaneko explained how to work the washing machine,

Nanase was unable to find any reference to the smell in her mind.

I wonder if she's got used to it, thought Nanase. That was the only explanation. After years and years, the stench must have completely lost its offensiveness. And Koichiro and all the rest of the family must be as oblivious to the smell as Kaneko is. There is no way that anyone aware of the stench could possibly put up with it.

An animal-like scent, acid mixed with saccharine. One might be able to block it out if one got used to it. But for those encountering the smell for the first time, it was so intolerable that it brought on nausea and headaches.

"I'll leave you to it. While you're at it, you can clean up the living room." There was no need to read Kaneko's mind; her delight at not having to do the washing showed clearly on her face. She went off, dangling a large shopping basket on her arm.

Nanase could not believe her eyes: there were nine loads of washing. Even with a family of thirteen, this is ridiculous, she thought. It's not as if it rained yesterday. With this much laundry every day, the washing machine isn't going to hold up much longer.

After Nanase got the washing started, she straightened up the living room and swept the floor. While she was working, she put together the pieces of Kaneko's mental make-up she had already glimpsed and gradually came to an understanding of her. Kaneko's eleven children hadn't made her the way she was. She was a born slob!

The living room, the kitchen – everywhere was dirty. Inside the cupboards, plates and cups not normally used were piled up in a jumble and covered with dust. The bowls by the sink had grains of rice hardening inside. Kaneko probably hadn't bothered to scrub them, but had just soaked them in water and wiped them. Rice starch had congealed on the tips of a dozen chopsticks standing in the drainer. Undoubtedly, Kaneko had just run them under water for a second.

Nanase was appalled. What ordinary housewife could put up with such filth? Probably her natural sloppiness had got worse by having to look after all these children. Before now, Nanase had worked for two or three families with close to ten members, but she had never come across anything like this. Come to think of it, having conceived eleven children was in itself a good indication of Kaneko's carelessness.

While Nanase was hanging up the washing in the backyard, she noticed that the sky was overcast. When she had peeked inside the drawers earlier, there was hardly any spare underwear. Actually, none at all would be a better way to put it. Probably whose underwear was whose was a moot point; she couldn't even find any belonging to Koichiro. What would happen if it rained tonight? Nanase shuddered at the thought. Most likely Kaneko wouldn't care.

The two girls and the boy in elementary school returned home and stared curiously at Nanase. Only the sixth-grader, Ayako, introduced herself. Nanase peered into their juvenile minds and saw immediately that they all had their father's amiable, easy-going nature. Whether they were as messy as their mother, she couldn't tell, but if their clothes were anything to go by, they were indifferent to dirt. Most likely, the other children were the same, Nanase concluded.

In an ordinary household, the children would want an after-school snack, but they seemed to realize there wouldn't be anything and didn't even bother to open the refrigerator. The only food inside was dried fish and garlic.

After the children got some spending money from Koichiro in the store and went out to play, the vegetable man came to deliver Kaneko's order. The kitchen table was buried under the vegetables – six turnips, three Chinese cabbages, twenty heads of lettuce and fifteen cucumbers.

In the evening the junior-high- and high-school-aged children came home one after another, but Kaneko had yet to return. She was probably gabbing with somebody somewhere when dinner has to be prepared, thought Nanase, who had no idea how the household was run. Of course, in this family there might be no need to worry about such things. But when she thought of having to prepare a meal for thirteen people, she was bound to feel anxious.

"Sorry I'm late."

Kaneko returned with three kilograms of beef, five loaves of bread, a pound of butter and other small items

36

inside her basket. It was already getting dark. The smaller children had got home long before and were watching TV in the living room, whining that they were hungry. What could she have been thinking of, Nanase wondered as she peered into her mind. Just as Nanase imagined, Kaneko had met a neighbourhood friend from her school days, and they had been chatting in a coffee shop by the station. Still dwelling on their conversation, Kaneko half-heartedly went about dinner – a large quantity of tasteless food. When dinner was ready, the two eldest sons, one a company employee, the other a college student, returned. Although the family was relatively well off, it seemed to be the policy not to give the children much pocket money and to insist that they eat dinner at home.

Nanase predicted that when the thirteen family members gathered around the table, they would be as noisy as a beehive, but the only commotion to speak of came from the smaller children arguing about what TV show to watch. They were no different from an ordinary small family – if anything, they were even quieter. The older children, junior high school and above, didn't pay much attention to Nanase, even though she was the family's first maid; they just ate in silence. Koichiro was the same.

Nanase peered into their minds: they were all absorbed in their personal problems as they mechanically plied their chopsticks. Nanase was impressed that they could consume so much awful food without complaining;

then again, when tasteless food becomes an everyday occurrence, one might no longer consider eating an act of pleasure. This could be the only explanation for the family's utter lack of interest in food.

That evening, after clearing the table, Nanase started to take in the washing, but it was still damp from the day's overcast sky. Kaneko told her to let it dry overnight. Against her better judgement, Nanase followed the order.

Nanase was the last to take a bath, but when her turn came, the water was covered with white scum. She couldn't bring herself to get into the tub, and so she made do by washing herself with cold water from the tap.

That night her head ached from the stench and she couldn't get to sleep. Every hour a bad dream would wake her up.

She dreamt that she was in the corner of a kitchen somewhere. She was squatting, trying with her scratchy tongue to scrape off grains of hardened rice stuck to the bottom of a chipped, dust-covered bowl. The taste was so terrible she woke up in a cold sweat. She found the family cat, who had crawled into her bedding, sleeping on her chest. The cat's dream had invaded her consciousness. She chased the cat into the hallway, and carefully shut the sliding doors.

When Nanase went out into the backyard in the morning, the laundry was still damp from a drizzle during the night. Now she had to iron each article of clothing until it was dry.

When Nanase went to the bathroom, she was disgusted to find that somebody had used her toothbrush. Probably no one had his or her own toothbrush, so if a slightly newer one was lying around, no one would bother over whose it was. She could count only ten toothbrushes, of which two or three were worn beyond use. So at least five or six members of the family had to be sharing toothbrushes.

I better keep my toothbrush somewhere else, thought Nanase. That morning she brushed her teeth with her finger.

As Kaneko was busy preparing breakfast, Nanase worked on the ironing. In the meantime, the children woke up and got dressed. Her ironing could not keep up with them. The children would come to the room, strip off their underwear, and grab the underwear that Nanase had just ironed. Some of the children, who couldn't wait for her to finish the ironing, would forage through the discarded underwear for the cleanest one they could find. They'd sniff the articles one by one, and put on whatever didn't smell too bad.

The junior-high and high-school children woke up and started fighting over the socks their elder brothers had discarded. One child played the clown by taking a big whiff and pretending to faint.

Soon the whole room began to stink. Nanase's head ached, and she felt like throwing up.

I'm going to fight this smell, Nanase resolved. I have to do something to rid the house of it. It's as if the family is stagnating in a stench that none of them can perceive.

After all the children except the two youngest had left, Nanase and Kaneko started on the breakfast dishes. According to Kaneko, the children weren't particularly smart, but they weren't particularly stupid either. These days, however, being on the slow side was an advantage over being too smart. This was Kaneko's strange view of life.

Kaneko spoke disjointedly, flitting from one topic to another without any logical connection. To avoid a repetition of the previous day's mishap, Nanase kept her latch fastened as much as possible, but did allow herself to glimpse into Kaneko's mind. The illness Koichiro had mentioned was actually a lie Kaneko had told him so she could hire a maid and do even less.

Kaneko had no interest in her husband, in making money, in housework, in her children or in her children's future. Her thoughts lacked any cohesiveness, and she had no clear-cut goals in life beyond wanting it easy. In a way these attempts to live on a pure, animal-like level were indicative of a feminine, almost too feminine, intellectual and emotional state – but actually, she was stuck at a more primitive and dishonest spiritual level. Daily drudgery had stripped her consciousness of the all-important mother instinct. Kaneko herself was not totally unaware that she was more negligent than the average housewife, but she justified it by convincing herself that she had an "optimistic" nature, and by bragging so to her friends.

Koichiro had a second income from selling land. When he left for the ward office to register some property, Kaneko had to mind the store. Nanase resolved to give the house a thorough cleaning and get at the roots of the stench.

There were any number of rooms. The bigger ones had been divided in half and the closets remodelled, so the children of high-school age and above had their own rooms.

All of the rooms were filthy. Except for the eldest daughter's, they looked as if they hadn't been cleaned in a month. Layers of dust had collected underneath the desks; sheets and blankets were covered with stains; pillowcases glistened with grease.

The college boy's bed was especially bad; under the mattress were dozens of nude photos that had been cut out of men's magazines. Underwear that had been used to wipe bodily fluids, and that were now as hard as a board, had been crumpled into balls and shoved underneath the bed. Nanase shuddered. She knew men relieved themselves sexually in various ways, but because the underwear was giving off such a horrendous odour, she could not ignore it.

She discovered similar things in the high-school boys' rooms. She gathered everything together and stuffed it all into paper bags which she then discarded in a plastic rubbish container. Then she scrubbed her hands with soap again and again.

From under the junior-high-school boy's desk, she unearthed a lunch box. It seemed to have been lying there for ages; when she cautiously opened the lid, she found it covered with a purple mould.

The washing machine was running constantly. Even after four loads of the underwear and shirts the children had discarded that morning, she still had the sheets and pillowcases to do. Nanase kept going.

At last, the cleaning was done, but the stench still hadn't gone. The stink seemed to have permeated the house itself; all Nanase could do now was wash the walls, posts and ceilings. She heaved a sigh. Her headache was becoming chronic. If I ever get over this headache, she smiled to herself, I won't be able to smell the odour either.

Partly in an attempt to forget the pain, she continued to work feverishly, all the while trying to keep her mind a blank. In the meantime the smaller children returned home and stared wide-eyed at their rooms, clean almost beyond recognition.

"Wow, who did this?"

Although they were clearly impressed, Nanase instantly picked up on a slightly critical note emanating from their consciousnesses. What could they be criticizing, she wondered with a start. Since they were children's minds with no well-formed thoughts or images, she wasn't sure what they meant, but she was put a bit on guard.

How would the older children react when they found their rooms cleaned? She braced herself for their return.

Just as she expected, that evening the college son came into the kitchen and asked Nanase nonchalantly if she was the one who had cleaned his room. When Nanase nodded, he gave her a twisted smile. It was a clumsy attempt to mask his hostility.

"Is that so? Uh, thanks."

Obvious hostility.

Why the hell doesn't she mind her own business? Did she know what I used the crumpled-up underwear for? There were nude photos in the same spot, so she must suspect something. She's only an eighteen-year-old girl, so she wouldn't know about a guy jerking off. Still, I wonder if she figured it out? Interfering bitch!

Of course, for him, Nanase was an invader who had disturbed his private sanctum.

Although the eldest son and the high-school boys didn't directly ask who had cleaned their room, they too began to harbour bad feelings towards Nanase. The night before there had been no hint of hostility in their consciousness; now she could clearly make out both their guilt at having their sordid secrets revealed and their inferiority complex towards cleanliness – that is, towards Nanase herself. In his thoughts, the eldest son was calling her "Peeping Tom".

This hostility reached a peak when the family gathered around the dinner table. To a third party without telepathic powers, the large household would probably have seemed the picture of a "wholesome" family. Even if one could perceive that this harmony was superficial, no one could have noticed any difference between this night's meal and all the other dinners up until now. But Nanase could tell that a major change had taken place in the Jimba family's collective consciousness. Nanase had exposed something hidden in their subconscious: the family's filth.

Thanks to their common mind and metabolism they had submerged themselves in a mire, their filth enveloped in a comfortably tepid stench. Now that this filth had been exposed, it pushed its way towards the surface of their consciousness. And the instigator of all this was none other than the eighteen-year-old maid who had arrived the day before.

The smaller children, influenced by the strange silence overtaking the dinner table, were making attempts in their confusion to maintain normal behaviour patterns.

"Thanks to Nana, the house has got really clean."

When Kaneko forced out the compliment, several of the children stiffened and stopped eating for a moment. Koichiro gave some automatic response. Then a definitive silence took over. The dining room filled with ill will towards Nanase.

You think you're better than us because you're clean. Leaving only the nude photos! What a bitch!

You want to make us feel inferior. Maybe I'll rape you. Then you'll be just like us.

Soon the ill will of the children began to turn back onto themselves in their own filth, and then onto their filthier family, for having made them this way.

Mum's at fault for being such a slob. Dad lets Mum get away with murder.

Hatred among the family, suppressed until now, began to flare up.

I'm filthy, I probably look like a pig to the maid. I am a pig.

Then, as if by common agreement, they began to recall graphically the various filthy acts they had committed in the past.

Kaneko alone remained unaware of her own sloth; her only concern was that Nanase had found out about her children. She was worried that Nanase would spread rumours about the family. She started recalling the various incidents when she had discovered her children's dirty ways. Kaneko knew better than anyone else about her children's filthiness.

The episodes unfolding in Kaneko's consciousness were so gross that Nanase felt like screaming. She quickly tried to fasten her latch. But she couldn't. She was mesmerized.

The Jimba family's filth-ridden consciousness had been whipped into a whirlpool that was sucking

Nanase in. The images floating in the minds of the entire family, the mental landscapes dotted with filth, the memories full of scum – these were assaulting Nanase non-stop as they released an ever-greater stench.

In the past, I did something much dirtier. I'm lucky she didn't find that *out. I wonder if she looked inside my drawers? Come to think of it, I once did something really disgusting. Then there was the time… Come to think of it… Come to think of it…*

These incidents full of excrement and bodily fluids were enough to make one's hair stand on end. Now they were surging full force into Nanase's consciousness, clashing with each other inside of her.

She could take it no longer.

Nanase got up and slowly walked into the hall.

The colour drained from her face as she ran into the bathroom. She threw up. She felt as if her stomach was going to burst. She couldn't stop vomiting.

"I see. Well, of course…"

When Nanase asked to leave her job, Koichiro was momentarily taken aback. As he mulled over various things – keeping up appearances, salary and so on – he let his eyes wander off into space and sighed.

I guess she couldn't stand the filth. That must be it. After all, she threw up in the bathroom.

Koichiro, like Kaneko, was concerned that Nanase would start rumours about how dirty the Jimbas were.

Koichiro knew that for a family with unmarried daughters it would be fatal if word got around that they had a "dirty kitchen". But what he hadn't realized until Nanase came was just how filthy his family really was.

Since Nanase wasn't going to explain why she wanted to quit and since Koichiro felt unable to press her for a reason, he was compelled to come up with some excuse himself. Sweating nervously, he offered an ingenuous substitution.

"I can't blame you. We're a family of thirteen. Any ordinary girl would have baulked just on hearing that. Anyway, you've done as much as you could. Really, you've done a good job. It's been short, but, honestly, you've done a good job."

Koichiro's candidness had flown off somewhere; all he could think about now was maintaining appearances. As if imploring her, he kept on and on with this meaningless repetition.

3

*In Quest of
Youth*

Nanase had been working at the Kawaharas' for two weeks, but she had yet to have any "human contact" with the family in the ordinary sense of the term. There hadn't even been any conversation to speak of, just high-handed orders which Nanase had carried out mechanically. Of course, this arrangement suited Nanase perfectly.

The family consisted only of the husband, Hisao, and Yoko, his wife.

In spite of this lack of human contact, in a mere two weeks Nanase had been greatly influenced by Yoko's personality and thoughts.

Yoko had an incredibly strong character. Nanase had worked as a live-in maid in a number of homes, but she had never come across a housewife with a personality like this.

At first Nanase hadn't realized that she had been "influenced"; she simply thought that, overwhelmed by Yoko's powerful ego, she was in a temporary state of shock. But two weeks later, when she went over her own mental processes, she could clearly detect Yoko's unique thought patterns.

That day as well, slightly after noon, Yoko, without one wasted word, flung her orders at the diminutive Nanase.

"Mr Kawahara should be home at seven tonight. Have his dinner ready. Just broil some meat and fry some vegetables. I won't be needing any. Take out his brown winter suit and iron it. If he asks, tell him I'll be back home at nine. Now that's only if he asks."

This abrupt manner of speaking suited the tall and heavily made-up Yoko; oddly it even had the opposite effect and made her seem more feminine.

However, Yoko's thought processes, which the curious Nanase had allowed to flow uninterrupted into her own mind, were extremely logical – one might even say mannish.

Yoko had not the least personal interest in Nanase. When she gave her orders, she would also be thinking about how to get her point across effectively, and how to make efficient use of the girl. Yoko's thoughts were linked together like an intricate chemical formula, the patterns changing shape moment by moment. Even Nanase, who had been exposed to any number of superior intelligences, was astounded at these prism-like refractions and dispersions.

It was only natural that under the influence of this strong personality, Nanase would grow more receptive to Yoko's consciousness. In time, Nanase became able to read Yoko's mind even at a distance.

When Nanase had turned ten, a few years after she had become aware of her telepathic powers, she noticed that while some people were weak, others emitted great inner strength. She discovered this when she'd undo her latch and peer into people's minds, only to find some consciousness coming at her full force.

Often this was because the person's mental make-up bore a close resemblance to Nanase's – in the case of a relative, for example – or because the person was emanating some strong feeling such as jealousy, love or desire. All the same, there did exist a few people whose inner will was at all times powerful. Yoko Kawahara, for example.

After Yoko drove off in her ivory-coloured sports car, Nanase took down from the top of the wardrobe the box with Hisao's three suits. The suit she was to iron looked as if it had been made three years ago. Hisao was a graduate of a top university and was on an elite career track in government service, so he could not neglect his personal appearance. Yet for some reason his wardrobe was small, and almost all of his summer suits looked old. Maybe, Nanase wondered, he's trying to tell Yoko in an indirect way not to be such a spendthrift.

The Kawaharas lived in a middle-class Western-style home on the outskirts of a new town. Nearby was a junction of the highway, which led to other small towns and the city centre. Yoko would always drive her sports car onto the highway, and Nanase would always follow Yoko's mind as she sped off to the city.

"I wonder how far I can follow her today."

This day as well, Nanase was chasing after Yoko as she mechanically did the ironing. Although Nanase tried to convince herself that she was doing this to test the limits of her power, the truth was that she wanted to observe Yoko's consciousness for as long as possible. Of course, before Yoko even left the house, Nanase knew where she was going and whom she was meeting. She was going to shop in the city and, while there, might look up her young boyfriend. Or she was planning to look up her young boyfriend and, while about it, might go shopping. In Yoko's consciousness, these two objectives were intricately entangled, leaving Nanase unable to determine which one was more important. For Nanase, this kind of refracted psychology was what fascinated her about Yoko. Even now, as her thoughts gradually faded, these refractions continued.

Vogue, Young Pilot, Mackenzie – Which shop has got something good in, I wonder. The other day I spotted a nice suit in Vogue, so I'll check that out first. Only if I can't find anything will I try the other two shops. Decided.

Through her usual process, Yoko's decisions hardened inside her.

In which case, I should choose some place close to Vogue for my date with Osamu – college senior, intelligent, athletic, sensitive, introverted, easily manipulated, weak-willed.

Strangely enough, Nanase's power was unaffected by obstacles. Even if a series of walls were to block the way or if the subject was in an enclosed chamber like an automobile, Nanase's telepathy was as strong as if there were no barriers. The one thing that did affect her power, however, was distance.

After Yoko had gone about eight kilometres down the highway, her telepathic messages suddenly weakened; from there on Nanase could only pick up fragments.

Tsuganuma Imperial Hotel. Nishikuromine Villa.
Which one...
Some place inconspicuous...

Yoko's thoughts vanished from Nanase's mind.

Nanase sighed. Still, that's not too bad, she muttered to herself, ignoring the real reason behind the sigh. Yesterday I lost her at five kilometres.

Actually, the psychology of an unfaithful wife was in itself nothing particularly new to Nanase.

Just as Yoko said, Hisao came home at seven precisely. Unless he had some business to attend to, he'd invariably return at seven so he could watch the evening news.

After finishing dinner in front of the TV, Hisao finally noticed that Yoko wasn't home. However, he didn't ask Nanase where she had gone. He also dismissed her as an eighteen-year-old kid.

Humph. So she's running around with some boy again. At thirty-seven, no less. Wait, or is she thirty-eight?

What was upsetting Hisao was neither jealousy nor worry over his wife's extravagances. His only concern was that his colleagues and superiors might learn of her affairs.

When Nanase first read Hisao's mind, she rather simplistically decided that he was an unfeeling man, and attributed Yoko's affairs to his coldness. But now she thought that the truth might be more complicated.

Nanase saw the two of them as thoroughgoing individualists, unlike any other couple she knew. Up until now Nanase had thought of individualism as a mere term bandied about by average intellectual couples to maintain an outward harmony and offer some justification for their actions.

After dinner, Hisao continued staring at the TV as he lingered over fruit and coffee. In his consciousness, criticism of his wife, unrelated to the TV show, would appear from time to time. While Nanase cleared the table, she peered curiously into Hisao's mind. She was interested in how someone other than herself would evaluate Yoko.

Yoko's logical thoughts were all closely related to her own actions. However, while Hisao's thoughts were also logical, they were divorced from reality and were almost entirely conceptual judgements of others. For this reason, it was difficult for Nanase to feel very positive towards Hisao.

Nanase could not put up with someone passive being critical of a person of action. For Nanase, this was the consciousness of an old person or a defeatist. Even if the action was – like a spouse's infidelity – the kind that was not to be admired, she did not see why a person who had lost his youthful energy had the right to criticize it.

It's about time she acted her age.

Doesn't she realize how foolish a middle-aged woman looks when she behaves like a young girl?

She's so intelligent, and yet seems to have no clear idea of herself.

She's only a woman, after all.

Tonight I'm going to say something to Hisao, thought Nanase. She could identify with Yoko, who was trying to live life to the fullest, and she had a strong desire to defend her.

Nanase did not even consider the consequences of such a defence. Actually, she even thought it might be better if the couple started arguing in the open. She could no longer stomach the way Hisao was content to criticize Yoko only in his mind.

She might be reprimanded later by Yoko, but even though Hisao hadn't asked her anything, when the clock struck eight, she acted as if she had suddenly remembered.

"Oh. Mrs Kawahara said she'd be home at nine."

"Humph. Nine o'clock?" For a moment Hisao looked as if he was going to laugh sardonically.

As usual she's probably made up like a young girl.

"Mrs Kawahara is so attractive," said Nanase without missing a beat. "And she's so youthful."

She was acting out the role of an innocent girl captivated by her mistress. Hisao immediately sensed Nanase's feelings.

What's this? She's on my wife's side?

He slowly looked up and stared at Nanase.

Come to think of it, Yoko acts just like an eighteen-year-old girl.

For the first time, Hisao was thinking of Nanase as a woman. And Nanase could tell from the way he was looking her over that he did not find her in the least attractive.

She's so skinny. Nothing but skin and bones. She has no sex appeal. Young girls these days are all like that. What's worse, the media is playing up this image. Fashion models – they're all the same. That's why the styles popular nowadays are just for this type. And Yoko forces herself to wear the clothes. It's so stupid. Why can't a middle-aged woman take pride in the maturity of her body? What's so great about the body of an undeveloped chit of a girl?

Images of buxom beauties – in particular, motherly women of the kind Rembrandt and Renoir liked to paint – paraded through Hisao's mind.

I'm sure those artists never showed any interest in skinny girls.

Nanase picked up on Hisao's strong Oedipus complex.

"I can see why you think she's pretty but..." – Hisao turned back to the TV and spoke slowly – "that's not the beauty of a middle-aged woman."

As soon as he said it, he reproached himself for having taken the girl seriously.

"Bring me a cup of tea in my study," he said, somewhat embarrassed, as he stood up.

When Nanase brought his tea, Hisao, his eyes focused on an administrative instruction manual lying open on his desk, was still thinking intently about middle-aged beauty.

She shouldn't wear ready-made clothes. They're all designed for a teenager's waist. But she thinks it's dowdy to have her clothes tailored, so she runs around buying outfits she can't wear without using a belt or something. Which is even more unbecoming.

Behind Hisao's logic lay the memory of a recent humiliation. He had been shopping in a department store for a pair of summer slacks, but couldn't find anything without a youthful cut and narrow waist; a young clerk, spotting his confusion, had smiled at him condescendingly.

Why should a sophisticated middle-aged couple with economic means run around buying ready-made clothes designed for the young at the expense of elegance and a fully developed femininity? It's subordination to the youth. Am I wrong? Only by having your clothes tailored can you free yourself from these popular youthful crazes and, as a mature human being, assert your own perfected individuality.

The more Hisao repeated his thinking, the more Nanase began to sense the desperation of someone about to lose his own youth. In fact, Hisao had little interest in clothes, and behind his insistence on "a wardrobe suitable for middle age" some subconscious force must have been at work unconnected with criticizing Yoko.

When a fragment of Hisao's logic overflowed the study into the dark hallway, Nanase smiled wryly to herself.

She had been watching TV for a while in the living room when the telephone in the corner rang.

Nanase picked it up. "The Kawahara residence."

"Oh Nana? It's me." It was Yoko.

According to the wall clock, it was exactly nine o'clock.

"I've had an accident," said Yoko.

"Oh my." Nanase held her breath. She couldn't read thoughts over the phone.

"It's nothing serious. Tell my husband I'll be home a little late." Her manner was as confident as always.

"Are you hurt?"

"*I'm* all right. So long." She hung up.

Nanase lost her usual composure. Judging by the way Yoko had said "I'm all right", someone else must have been injured.

Yoko had a racer's licence and until now had probably never had an accident. Had the accident been beyond her control? Or had Yoko been in an unstable mental state?

No, that couldn't be. Nanase denied the idea vehemently. Nanase didn't even want to think that Yoko, with her unbending personality, could ever be disturbed enough to commit a driving error.

When she reported the news to Hisao in the study, his eyes widened a bit as he turned around.

"An accident, you say?"

So she finally did it. It only stands to reason – the way she acts, like a kid racing about in a sports car.

"But... uh... she said it wasn't anything serious."

"Is that so?" Hisao nodded. "Then there's probably nothing to worry about."

Since Yoko was always honest with him, Hisao had no reason to doubt what she said, but in this case he seemed to be eager to reassure himself. He did love Yoko in his own way but, perversely enough, he could only show it by criticizing her inwardly.

For a long time Hisao and Nanase faced each other in silence.

Hisao was mulling over what stance to take towards Yoko. No matter how much he criticized her in his mind, when they were actually face to face, he'd end up being nice to her. Tonight, however, he seemed to be leaning the other way.

Nanase realized that it was she who had provoked him into it.

"I'll wait up for her in the living room," said Nanase, shutting the study door.

Hisao didn't even seem to hear her; still in a daze, he was thinking over what to say to Yoko.

It was after ten when Nanase finally picked up Yoko's consciousness as she returned from the freeway. Her mind was unusually confused, making it difficult for Nanase to understand what had happened. Clearly Yoko was tired and in ill humour.

This is a fine mess, thought Nanase.

With the proud Yoko in a bad mood, she was bound to blow up at Hisao if he spoke arrogantly to her. As Yoko's consciousness became more and more intelligible, Nanase's agitation kept on increasing.

Yoko had been stood up by Osamu, the boyfriend she had dismissed as indecisive and weak-willed. Then in Vogue she had been unable to find a dress that fitted. After that, she had gone alone to see a movie, became irritated by the insipid film, and on the way back had run into a drunk who had dashed onto the road. She hadn't been going fast, and the drunk didn't seem to have been injured, but even so, she had been carted off to the nearest police station and given a hard time.

"I feel so sorry for her," murmured Nanase with a sigh. What a cruel day it must have been for a woman with Yoko's self-esteem.

When Yoko returned, she was exhausted, her face pale almost beyond recognition.

"See. Even if you think you can drive a car like some kid, your responses have dulled. That's why you hit him."

After coming into the living room and hearing the details from Yoko, Hisao launched into his rebuke, harbouring a subconscious desire to have Nanase hear it as well.

"He was drunk," Yoko replied, irritated. "It was his fault. Otherwise they'd have never let me go home so soon."

But in spite of what she said, Hisao seemed to have made an impact.

I wonder if my driving really has got worse because of my age. Come to think of it, in the past, with that much distance, I probably could have avoided him.

Then she immediately rejected the thought.

No, the accident happened because I was overwrought today.

Hisao, oblivious to what his wife was thinking, staunchly continued his attack.

"Do you think you can regain your youth by driving a sports car designed for kids? You're just fooling yourself. And don't forget you're a woman. A woman's driving skills decline much faster than a man's. Sure, young people do have the highest accident rate, but their accidents are the result of speeding. Accidents by the middle-aged are clearly due to weakened responses. Young people are still minors, so they can't be held responsible for their actions. As a middle-aged woman, you've got to have a sense of social responsibility."

He's gone far enough, thought Nanase anxiously. She was hoping that Yoko would lash back. But tonight Yoko had lost her energy. With nothing to stop him, Hisao's criticisms dragged on interminably.

"Let me go to sleep. I'm tired," Yoko broke in suddenly.

Who would have believed that Yoko would give in so easily? But Yoko meant what she said.

Why does he keep harping on about youth? *Perhaps he's not in love with* youth *the way I am. Or maybe he's jealous of my youthfulness.*

Depressed as she was, Yoko was trying to fathom her husband's feelings.

"Then go to sleep," said Hisao. "But I want you to give up your sports car."

Yoko seemed taken aback by Hisao's uncharacteristic tone.

"Is that an order?"

For a moment Hisao's usual timidity returned and he flinched. But then he answered emphatically: "That's right, it's an order."

All that night Nanase was disturbed by Yoko's intense thoughts emanating from her bedroom. Yoko was trying to heal her wounds by reinforcing her ego. She had suffered a traumatic blow by being told she was no longer young. Once she had been the centre of the world, the essence of youth itself. For her, youth was the lead in a lavish production, whereas middle age was only a supporting role. So for Yoko to acknowledge herself as middle-aged would be the same as throwing away her self-esteem.

Have I been cast aside by Osamu?

Have I lost my hold on youth?

Is this the end of my era?

Will I be forced to play bit parts from now on?

She shuddered and denied it all vehemently.

If that's the case, I'm better off dead.

Yoko seemed quite incapable of getting to sleep. Which meant that Nanase couldn't sleep either, for she was unable to fasten her latch and cut off Yoko's mind. The intense pressure this consciousness was exerting on her would not allow her to ignore it.

The next morning, two hours after Hisao left for work, Yoko got up.

"Could you get me a cup of coffee?"

When Nanase peered into Yoko's mind from across the kitchen table, she learnt that Yoko had undergone another violent shock that morning on discovering how utterly worn and aged she looked in the mirror. Her face, haggard from lack of sleep, was unmistakably that of a pathetic woman desperately clinging to her youth. Her thirty-eight years, typified by tired skin and flabby cheeks, could no longer be denied.

It occurred to Nanase that Hisao was the one who had driven Yoko into this awful state. Up until now, Yoko had used her powerful ego and quick brain to block out her age. Hisao was wrong to have reminded her of it.

And yet there was also a more sensible voice inside Nanase saying that Hisao was in the right. Nanase for some reason did not want to hear it – choosing to defend Yoko's devotion to youth, even if her actions were immoral, simply because of the empathy she felt towards another woman. What was wrong with trying to keep a hold on youth? Wasn't it human to fear death?

Suddenly Nanase noticed that Yoko was staring into her face with a strange gleam in her eyes. Yoko seemed to be devouring Nanase's creamy skin glistening in the morning sun, while in her thoughts she was ripping the skin off with her sharp nails and attaching it to her own face.

I want her skin. I want her youth. I want her inexperience, her vulnerability. I want her healthy stupidity.

While Yoko's judgement of her as inexperienced and stupid was obviously off the mark, Nanase found Yoko's weird fantasy so frightening that she was having trouble keeping calm.

Luckily, Yoko's thoughts soon moved to Osamu.

I wonder if he really was avoiding me? Why don't I call him? He's probably home now.

Nanase wanted to yell at her to stop. She couldn't stand to watch Yoko telephone the young boy who had rejected her and try to regain his love by chiding him coquettishly. But Yoko went to the living room, picked up the receiver and started dialling. Nanase was relieved to find in Yoko's thoughts not the least desire to play the coquette. The problem was how Osamu would react. Yoko was going to show him who was boss.

Osamu picked up the phone right away. She could hear his voice through Yoko's consciousness.

"Osamu? It's me." Yoko spoke calmly.

"Oh…" He was at a loss for an answer. He probably never dreamt that she would call. He too must have been aware of Yoko's pride.

"You didn't show up yesterday," said Yoko, her tone harsh.

"I'm sorry," he apologized immediately. He seemed nervous. "I was thinking of calling you, but I knew I shouldn't call you at home and—"

"You can give me your excuses later," said Yoko flatly. "At one o'clock I want you to come to where we arranged to meet yesterday."

She wasn't going to take no for an answer, so after some hesitation, he agreed. He was clearly afraid of her.

What's the point of going out with such a fraidy cat, thought Nanase, and at that very moment Yoko was thinking the same thing. Yoko was meeting him for her own sake, not for that of their relationship. They'll end up hurting each other, predicted Nanase uneasily. Yoko seemed to be in an even worse state than the night before, and Nanase was afraid – both for Yoko and for herself.

As Yoko got ready to leave, she thought over how best to approach Osamu so she could get at his true feelings. Slightly past noon, ignoring Hisao's order, she drove off in her sports car without a word to Nanase about when she'd be back or what chores to do. Yoko was hardly the type to put up with jolting suburban trains or rude taxi drivers.

As she cleaned the kitchen, Nanase pursued Yoko's consciousness. Once Yoko entered the highway, she started picking up speed – obviously in reaction to Hisao's criticisms.

I'm not going to take this lying down. I'm not the kind of person who will give up driving a car and wearing ready-made clothes because they're supposedly not suitable for me.

She'd better be careful, thought Nanase, who could only clench her fists, petrified. Yoko was speeding at 170 kilometres per hour in the overtaking lane. True, there were few cars on the road, but only once before, a number of years ago, had she gone so fast. Nanase had a mental picture of Yoko's field of vision and the speed was making her head spin. A distant trailer in the left lane was getting closer moment by moment.

When there were only ten metres between her and the trailer, it suddenly veered into the overtaking lane at eighty kilometres per hour to pass a small automobile. Yoko hadn't seen the automobile. Nanase let out a cry.

At once Yoko could see the back of the trailer looming larger.

All right.

Yoko bit her lips.

Since middle-aged drivers never have accidents speeding… I don't care if I die.

For one moment Yoko's field of vision went pitch black, then a panorama unfolded in her consciousness.

Five seconds later her consciousness began to diffuse. At the far side of the widening crack lay death.

Nanase screamed. This was the first time she had seen death. Death was the colour of nothingness. The colour of nothingness was neither black nor even the colour of empty space, but, quite simply, the colour of nothingness. It was a colour so frightening that Nanase feared it might drive her insane. All alone in the house, she stood by the kitchen table, fists clenched and flinging her arms about violently, as if to expel a nightmare before her eyes. And all the while she kept on screaming hysterically.

After Yoko's death, during her funeral and until Nanase left the Kawahara home, Hisao tried to convince himself that he was not responsible for her death. By trying to lay the blame on something other than himself, his complicated mental mechanism was suppressing and distorting a guilt that was dangerously close to surfacing in his consciousness.

Yoko was the victim of an aberrant cult of youth. In this modern era, which only recognizes products, amusements and culture for the young, middle-aged values have been debased. The middle-aged are made to feel superfluous and the young are resentful of getting older. The step after youth worship is the search for rejuvenation; the middle-aged are all slaves of this quest for youth. They detest conventions and clothing suited to their age, and insist on copying the young styles. Of course, they only end up making fools of themselves. Yoko was wrong. Turning middle-aged is not a banishment from youth; it's a mature human being's liberation from the insanities of youth. However, caught up in this era of youth worship, she was unable to perceive this. Even though her car, a product of this youth-idolizing age, has capacities too advanced for a middle-aged person, she was under the delusion that she had perfect control of it. She was killed by our modern age – this crazy age where the youth cult is running rampant. There's no doubt about it. No doubt about it. Because, you see, she too was taken in by these modern advertisements spouting their ridiculous elixirs for rejuvenation, and with an unswerving belief that as long as she had the desire she could maintain her youth for ever, she never even dreamt that she would be middle-aged. It was this frantic youth-centred age that made her think this way. There's no doubt about it. She was killed by our crazy modern society. Absolutely. Because, you see…

Because…

Because…

4

The Peach

The Kiryus lived in a neighbourhood that dated back before the war. It had probably been a fashionable area once, if the ornate carvings on the bay windows and balconies that could be glimpsed beyond hedges and lush gardens were anything to go by. But now most of the houses were run down, with the vaguely melancholic air of having been left behind by the times. For Nanase, who was accustomed to bright, new residential neighbourhoods, these houses, hidden beneath towering trees that had grown unchecked, seemed almost shabby.

The Kiryus' home was badly in need of repair. If they could afford a live-in maid, the family was by no means poor; yet they showed no interest in making any repairs. The house, both inside and out, was going to seed. The walls and ceilings were black with dirt, the wooden panelling was loose in places, all of the rooms were dark. The small maid's room that Nanase had been provided with did not even have a window, and the grimy walls and ceiling only made it that much worse. Even for Nanase, who was used to poorly lit rooms, the darkness was almost unbearable.

"This house is so run down," the members of the family would sometimes mutter, looking around as if suddenly remembering the fact. But no one ever suggested making repairs or calling in a carpenter. Obviously no one wanted the responsibility.

The head of the Kiryu household was fifty-seven-year-old Katsumi, who had retired two years earlier. Up until then his company, which manufactured steel pipes, had had a mandatory retirement age of sixty; then, like a bolt out of the blue, the retirement age was lowered to fifty-five. Katsumi was completely caught off guard by his forced early retirement, and he had still not got over the shock. In fact, it seemed to Nanase that his absent-mindedness, perhaps brought on by his retirement, was getting steadily worse.

Nanase had been working at the Kiryus' for only two months, but from reading Katsumi's mind, she knew that the goals he had carefully made for his retirement, along with the confidence that he could live out his remaining years at his own pace, had been cruelly smashed. She sensed the terrible emptiness brought on by his idle existence.

Katsumi was well aware that his family shunned him. At first they were attentive to his needs; now they thought nothing of treating him as so much excess baggage, with his loafing around the house all day with nothing to do. Even his wife, Teruko, found him a nuisance.

"Father's awful – he spies on us in our bedroom," Ayako, the daughter-in-law, told Nanase. As far as Nanase could tell from reading Ayako's mind, however, Ayako was really complaining about the lewd glances Katsumi gave her.

Ryuichi, Katsumi's eldest son, had just turned thirty and had already been promoted to section chief in charge of raw materials at a shipbuilding company. Of course, Ayako's desire to brag about her husband made her want to deprecate Katsumi all the more. And in fact, the image of Katsumi in Ayako's mind was that of a failure.

"Hey, could you get me some tea?" Katsumi would wander into the kitchen any number of times a day, sit down across from Nanase at the table and stare at her as she worked. This was probably the look he had given his daughter-in-law before Nanase had moved in, and it was so offensive that Ayako had cajoled Ryuichi into hiring a maid.

Katsumi's behaviour and – as Ayako pictured them in her thoughts – his lewd stares were even more disturbing to Nanase because she could see so clearly the struggle and repression in his consciousness. Still, it was a relief that whenever she was with Ayako, Katsumi's glances would stray in the daughter-in-law's direction.

At dinner time, Teruko, always in bed with some illness, would emerge from a back room, and the whole family would assemble in the dining room. There were six in all – Katsumi and his wife, Teruko; their elder son, Ryuichi, and his wife, Ayako; their younger son, Tadaji, a high-school senior; and their four-year-old grandson, Akira. They usually watched television, but occasionally someone would start a conversation. Then invariably they would end up criticizing, in a roundabout fashion, the idle ways of the head of the household, giving irresponsible – and hardly considerate – suggestions on how to reform him.

"You went into my room today, didn't you, Father?" Tadaji asked one evening, not bothering to disguise the accusation. A medicine commercial flashed onto the TV screen.

Tadaji had long suspected that when he wasn't home, his father would sneak into his room and go through his drawers and letters. But since he had no evidence, Tadaji had kept quiet. Now he just had to say something. It was obvious that his father had read a letter from a girl.

Horny bastard. Nothing better to do than nose around your son's room.

Tadaji despised his father for being so incompetent as to lose his job at the age of fifty-five. To him, this pot-bellied, slimy lecher who happened to be his father looked more like some out-of-work bum than a retired gentleman.

"Uh-huh." Judging from Tadaji's tone, Katsumi imagined that his son had proof for his accusation, so he didn't try to deny it. "I was looking for, uh, an interesting book to read."

What's so bad about a father going into his son's room? You're only in high school, smart-arse kid!

Even if Katsumi did feel a bit guilty for having read the letter from the girl, he was disgusted at being in so weak a position that he had to justify himself to his seventeen-year-old son.

Damn. Who's the head of this household anyway?

In these instances, Nanase would momentarily forget the dislike she felt towards Katsumi during the day and feel sorry for him. Since she herself was constantly reading minds, Katsumi's snooping around people's rooms seemed an innocent enough way to relieve his boredom.

After debating whether or not to defend Katsumi, Teruko decided to keep quiet. Tadaji was so stubborn that anything she might say in her husband's defence would only provoke the child even more. The end result would be the loss of Katsumi's parental authority. Once that happened, Ryuichi and, worse, his wife might start throwing their weight around. This was the one thing Teruko would not be able to put up with.

Of course, for Teruko, Katsumi had lost his authority as a husband a long time ago. For a number of years she had used illness as an excuse to deny him marital pleasures. Katsumi, at fifty-seven, was two years younger than her and still maintained the vigour of a carnivorous beast. Even now he would pursue her whenever he could. But Teruko, who had convinced herself that she had a body like a prune, could only feel an intense physical loathing towards him.

Recently Teruko had aged suddenly, her hair having turned grey. Her disgust for the way Katsumi clung to his youth, symbolized by his jet-black hair, made her more defiant. Oddly enough, she was trying to protect herself by ridiculing her husband for acting like a kid carried away with his sex drive. As Nanase saw it, these attempts at convincing herself of the benefits of turning old were really ways to block out her fear of death. Surely this pretence at sickliness was an unconscious escape into disease.

"You have too much time on your hands, Dad," said Tadaji sarcastically, though he had given up pursuing the matter of the letter. He knew that if he pressed his father too much, Teruko, in her role as mother, and Ryuichi, in his role as elder brother, would have to intervene on Katsumi's behalf.

Why don't you get another job? You were lording it over everyone as section chief all those years so you can't stomach the thought of starting as an underling at a new company. You don't want to go where you can't act high and mighty, so you lord it over us at home. Creep!

Tadaji's feelings towards his father resembled Ryuichi's. Ryuichi, however, realized that he hated Katsumi because they were so much alike. It depressed him to think that one day he might end up like his father; of course, he was also confident it would never happen to him. Even if he were forced to retire, he was convinced that he'd be able to find some reason to go on living.

What Ryuichi hadn't considered, though, was how he would go about finding this reason or what reason it might be. Ryuichi was keenly aware that a lowering of the retirement age was the general trend, and this was a constant worry to him. It was because he couldn't bear to see his father in his present state that he ridiculed him for being unable to do anything about it.

"Father, I've heard about a computer that in ten minutes can pick out the work best suited for you. Why don't you give it a try?" Ryuichi suggested casually. As he was, at least on the surface, softening Tadaji's attack, he was able to speak his mind.

I'm sure you'll find fault with the idea for one reason or another. Why don't you just go out and buy a woman? The nerve, giving my wife obscene looks. You old lecher! With your shiny, greasy forehead! In spite of your pent-up energy, all you can do is laze around. If you were really over the hill, I wouldn't care about looking after you.

Nanase, who had explored the psychologies of various families she had worked for, knew that hatred among close relations was nothing unusual. Still, Ryuichi's denunciation of his father, just because Ryuichi realized he would be in the same predicament himself one day, was more than she could take.

Katsumi, pretending to be watching a drama on TV, did not answer Ryuichi. But in his mind he was cursing his son's irresponsible proposition made under the guise of kindness.

Find a job from a machine? What a way to speak to your father. Treating me like a nuisance. If I'm so much in the way, why don't you all move out? You think you're so smart, but you don't have enough money to buy your own house! You're just living off your parents. I know you have your eyes on the money I got when I retired. You think I'd give any of it to you? You've got to be kidding. I'll spend it all. On whatever I feel like.

But Katsumi had so much money that he knew he could never spend it all, even if he found some expensive hobby. What could he do anyway? And even if he thought of something, he knew he wouldn't enjoy it.

As Nanase saw it, Katsumi's biggest problem was that he didn't know how to have a good time. Someone who knew how to enjoy himself would probably come up with a hobby that not only wouldn't cost any money, but might even turn a profit; this in itself could give him a reason to go on living.

But from the time Katsumi had entered his company up until the present – in other words, for the greater part of his life – he had never wanted to relax. He had lived only for his work, and since he thought of amusement as a kind of vice, he even considered it dangerous. So for him to lose his job was like being expelled from the Garden of Eden.

Various incidents that occurred at the time of his retirement were still floating around in Katsumi's mind. These were memories which had become concrete images and which Nanase had glimpsed any number of times in the two months she had worked here.

After he had been told of his retirement, he started putting more and more energy into his job. Then one day he was shocked to realize that the documents he was being asked to handle were gradually decreasing in number.

I broke down and cried.

He remembered the dazed feeling on the day he retired, when his underlings saw him off at the entrance showering him with lively cheers. Their shouts of "good luck" sounded like "get lost"; all he could feel was a burning humiliation.

My knees were shaking.

Then there was the time.

And the time…

And the time…

"You didn't enjoy deep-sea fishing, did you, Father?" asked Ayako. She had suggested he take up fishing, because it had been her own father's hobby.

"It just didn't suit me," Katsumi responded affably.

I can't understand why anyone would do something that boring. I felt so bored I wanted to weep.

Humph. If it's Ayako, he'll answer. Look at him making eyes at her.

What a lecherous smile! It sends shivers down my spine.

"Grandpa, it's not good for your body to loaf around the house," Akira piped in precociously. He was mimicking the way his parents would talk in their second-floor bedroom. Ryuichi and Ayako, caught off guard for a moment, glared at Akira and then nervously gauged Katsumi's reaction.

"Is that so? Is that so?" Katsumi stared at his grandson with the same drooling expression. He nodded a few times.

This adorable child was the reason why he didn't get angry at his son and daughter-in-law for the way they treated him. Obviously, if they moved out, he wouldn't be able to see Akira any more either.

"Stop saying 'Is that so?' over and over," Akira raised his voice, annoyed at being treated like a child. "You've got to get out of the house."

So even my grandson treats me like a nuisance. He's been taught by his parents.

Katsumi's smile vanished and he stared at Ryuichi and Ayako.

"You can't talk that way to Grandpa," scolded Ayako, who was making a show of being embarrassed.

"It's OK. He's only speaking the truth," said Teruko, chuckling to herself. She gave Akira an approving nod. She was well aware that as long as she was siding with their grandson, Katsumi would not get openly angry.

Serves you right!

Tadaji was laughing derisively inside.

Nanase was disgusted. Although she was about the same age as Tadaji, she could not find one thing she had in common with him. Taking into account the fact that he was a boy, he was still insensitive, rude, ill-tempered and severely stunted emotionally. This type of guy, she knew from her experiences in high school, would attract a lot of girls. But none of them would see him for what he really was; they would mistake rudeness for manliness. He was the kind of boy who often came up in girls' conversations, but Nanase couldn't care less.

"I would like to get a job," Katsumi said at last. He had said this so many times before, however, that his entire family could predict his next line: "But the best job I could get would be a security guard or a nightwatchman." Then he slowly looked over his family in a somewhat high-handed manner.

Even they wouldn't have the gall to tell me to be a security guard. And surely they're not going to suggest that I pay daily visits to an employment agency. I was a section chief. What if someone who worked under me saw me in a place like that?

Pompous stuffed shirt.

In spite of the fact he can't do anything.

Humph. He said himself that the only job he's capable of getting is a security guard or nightwatchman.

He's so incompetent, how could he ever have become section chief?

As if on cue, everyone started to revile him in their minds. It was like a hail of curses.

"But if you put your mind to it, I'm sure you could find something," Ryuichi quickly added. This too was a standard line.

No one in the family had any idea what the first two to three months of retirement were like for Katsumi. He had learnt in a matter of days how painful this long, long stretch of time with nothing to do would be, and in fact he had determinedly gone looking for a job every day.

But there was nothing suitable. There was no kind of work that he could throw himself into the way he had been doing up until then. An employment agency could probably find him some menial job, but he didn't consider such jobs to be real work. And anyway, his pride would not permit him to go to an employment agency.

It dawned on him that mandatory retirement was, in effect, the same thing as forcibly taking a job away from somebody. Even prisoners were better off. At least they didn't have any free time.

Katsumi's family, however, looked at the new lifestyle of the head of the household and concluded that he was having a grand old time of it. Katsumi knew what they were thinking. But he wasn't about to confess that he had seriously gone searching for work just after his retirement. It surprised Nanase that he was ashamed of this desire to work. His greatest fear was that a workaholic's need for a job would seem as base as the desire for food or women.

Nanase observed Katsumi's psychology with deep interest. At the same time, she had become preoccupied anew with her own extrasensory ability to read people's minds.

When she first realized she was telepathic, Nanase wanted to know why she had this special power and if there might be anyone else with the same ability. In junior high school, she secretly looked for books that might supply the answer. However, the only books she could find had titles like *Weird but True Tales*, *How to Be a Mind Reader* and *Strange Stories from around the World*. These, of course, were completely useless.

In high school, she systematically read all the books on psychology she could find. She also read general works by and about people claiming to have extrasensory powers. And she consumed parapsychological studies in English based on experimental research – especially works by the scholars J.B. Rhine, S.G. Saul and G. Schmeidler. But again she was unable to obtain any concrete answers.

The great majority of books on psychology did not so much as touch on the topic. If there was an occasional article, the tone was almost always sceptical. The books for general readers were bogus, written solely to titillate, and virtually all the important works of parapsychological research foundered at the experimental level.

Nanase despaired of ever finding a scientific explanation for her power. She gave up her search and accepted her ability simply as something that existed. Her power, she reasoned, was akin to an animal performing sexually without knowing the purpose of its action.

But now, through her observations of Katsumi Kiryu's emotional state, she had become interested in her ability once again. She no longer cared about scientific explanations; now her interest lay in finding out the limits and possibilities of her telepathic power. She wanted to see just how completely she could read Katsumi's mind. She had chosen him as a subject for an experiment in ESP.

A few days later Nanase noticed a change in Katsumi. The lewd glances he had given to Ayako were being directed solely at her. Ayako must have noticed the change as well. In the kitchen one day, she grinned and whispered into Nanase's ear: "Father seems to have taken a liking to you. You have my sympathies."

Ayako was relieved that her father-in-law's interest had strayed elsewhere, but at the same time she was more than a little jealous of Nanase. Why should she, in full possession of her feminine charms, take second place to this skinny wisp of a maid?

Nanase, however, couldn't care less about the all-too-female workings of Ayako's mind. What she really wanted to know was why she had become the sole object of Katsumi's attentions.

The image of Nanase in Katsumi's consciousness was that of a Chinese peach, its white skin tinged with pink. Katsumi had superimposed Nanase's youthful, creamy white flesh onto the glistening down of a sweet, juicy peach.

Why? Why me suddenly?

And why this poetic and symbolic image of a peach – so atypical for a middle-aged man? Nanase probed deeper into Katsumi's mind.

A popular magazine had recently published a special issue on the problems of the elderly, and Katsumi had come across the image of the peach in a bit of verse by an American poet.

The poem also used images of mermaids, the beach and a necktie, but it was the symbolic line about eating peaches that had left the most vivid impression on Katsumi, and he had transferred the erotic aspect of this image to the peach-like young girl in the midst of his family.

Katsumi's interest in his daughter-in-law stemmed only from erotic desire – a libido that sought out Ayako's ripe figure. No doubt his interest in Nanase also had its share of the erotic, but in this case desire was intricately bound up with the longing for lost youth, as symbolized in the poem, and with the perverted self-assertions of a man who felt that his retirement had estranged him from society. Katsumi also thought that to take advantage of the maid was hardly the same as to rape his own daughter-in-law. For all this, his desire for Nanase was far stronger and more complex.

Nanase sensed the danger. Katsumi was actually considering rape!

While Nanase might have had an interest in Katsumi's psychology, that did not mean, of course, that she felt any real sympathy for him. Nor was she about to be a victim to his sliminess. Just the thought of him assaulting her made her cringe in horror. But in fact, in Katsumi's consciousness, the image of rape was becoming more and more graphic.

Nanase had read that anyone confined in a monotonous environment for a long period of time will inevitably take a turn for the worse. If that was true, then it was only natural for Katsumi, a man who had thrown himself into his work his whole life, to lose his mental balance. Day by day, Nanase could see the danger closing in on her.

Until now Katsumi had used his work to assert and justify his existence. Only through his work was he able to feel confident that there was a bond between him and society at large. But with his retirement, all this had vanished, and his ego was on the verge of crumbling. He had his sights set on Nanase in an effort to regain his sense of self. By violating the peach-like virgin, he could justify his existence. Through her youth – through a *stranger*, who belonged not to his family but to the *outside world* – he could create once more a bond between himself and society.

The more Nanase raked through his consciousness and subconscious, the clearer it became that Katsumi's spirit had been driven into a corner from which there was no escape – and that she had become the only refuge for his ego. It was hopeless to try to divert his attention.

Nanase gritted her teeth. If she didn't quit, her only recourse was to tackle each dangerous incident as it happened.

The danger came earlier than expected.

Ryuichi, Ayako, Akira and Tadaji had taken advantage of a long holiday to make a trip to Kyushu. Even though they knew that Katsumi would use his wife's illness as an excuse not to go, no one even went through the motions of inviting him. Katsumi, his wife and Nanase were left behind in the house.

With his children gone, Katsumi put together his plan to assault Nanase. Teruko's bedroom was in the back of the house, while the maid's room was right next to the entrance hall. Even if Nanase screamed a little, it was unlikely that Teruko would hear her. She might even be too embarrassed to scream – after all, she was a virgin.

Nanase was amazed at the way Katsumi was thinking. He was like a criminal, egging himself on with one-sided calculations for the crime he was about to commit. But it was entirely conceivable that Teruko would not wake up no matter how much Nanase screamed. The insomniac Teruko regularly took sleeping pills, which she kept hidden from the family.

When evening came, the only defence Nanase could think of was to hammer a nail into the sliding doors of her room.

It was after one in the morning when Katsumi's bloated ego and sweaty feet headed slowly down the hall to the maid's room.

Once a woman's been raped, she's putty in a man's hands.

He was desperately trying to encourage himself by dredging up from memory his extremely meagre, juvenile and simplistic knowledge of women.

What's more, she's a virgin. Since I'll be her first man, all the better. No matter what she says, I can't waver. Girls these days are all talk. The worst would be if halfway through I let her talk me out of it. All I have to do is rape her, and she'll keep her mouth shut.

If she starts crying, I can't feel sorry for her. I don't care if she cries. I don't care if she gets angry – I'm going through with it.

Whatever Nanase said, he was determined not to listen. Whether she pleaded, cried or threatened, nothing would stop him now. He was going to possess her body by force. And Nanase knew only too well that he was strong enough to do it.

Nanase shivered. Why am I here? How stupid of me to stay when I knew what was coming.

Katsumi stopped in front of her sliding doors and renewed his determination.

All right. Do the job from start to finish, and don't say a word.

The nail on the sliding door proved utterly useless.

The next moment, Katsumi's bull-like, square-shouldered hulk became a black silhouette barring the way at the edge of Nanase's bedding. Nanase jumped up and retreated to the far side of the room.

The fluorescent light from the hall shone faintly into the tiny room. Nanase could not see Katsumi's face, but most likely he could see hers, pale and expressionless.

Even when his eyes caught her in her blue-striped pyjamas, Katsumi's mind did not register any erotic impulse. He was obsessed with a personal sense of mission to carry through to the end the violence he had planned for so long. For him, this was "work", which required inhumanity and brute strength, and which would bring him only an inkling of physical pleasure.

He felt no guilt about what he was about to do. Violating this peach-like virgin was "substitution behaviour", to take the place of searching for a new job, something he had failed at so miserably. It was an action far easier, far less humiliating, than looking for work. After all, taking advantage of the maid was a common practice dating from olden times. Even if word got out, his action would probably be considered less reprehensible than openly looking for a job.

But, in reality, when Katsumi faced Nanase, he was extremely agitated, in spite of all his encouragements.

Nanase knew that her chances were almost nil, but she pinned her hopes on the smallest of possibilities, and spoke to him in as calm a voice as she could muster.

"If you leave quietly now, I won't tell anybody."

Liar!

As expected, Katsumi vehemently denied her in his mind.

Now that I've forced my way into her room, I've got to finish the job. If I leave now, she'll blab it to anyone she can think of. Girls are like that.

This inner rebuttal only increased his desperation. He had become so worked up that he didn't notice how unvirginlike Nanase's calm was. This put Nanase at an extreme disadvantage.

Katsumi stepped onto the bedding and closed in on her.

Nanase gave up trying to talk to him, her mind feverishly searching for some way out of the situation. True, she did not place that much importance on her virginity. Be that as it may, there was no way she was going to put up with his taking her forcibly, as some kind of convenient substitution. Worst of all, she was afraid of the physical pain. In her consciousness she had already telepathically experienced the pain of a ruptured hymen, and she could tell he would be violent.

Katsumi tried to grab Nanase's arm. At the same time, his other hand reached for her shoulder. By intuiting each of his actions before they occurred, Nanase was able to escape him moment by moment. But once he pressed in on her, she was defenceless. He forced her down onto the bedding.

With Nanase's silken skin and breath now close at hand, Katsumi's lust grew. After years of abstinence, the feeling of the young girl's flesh beneath her pyjamas gave him an instant erection. Whatever Nanase might say, however she might resist, it was too late. His consciousness was at the peak of excitement.

In the midst of fighting Katsumi off, Nanase had an idea.

So far, she had appealed only to his reason. But now that his mind, which had been in an abnormal state to begin with, had reached such a frenzied pitch, she knew that any rational attempts to dissuade him would prove useless. In which case, why couldn't she use her power to drive him really berserk?

I *can* do it, thought Nanase.

However there was a risk involved – the risk of revealing to an unsuspecting world the power she had kept hidden so long.

But there was no time to lose. Katsumi had already stripped off her pyjamas and was yanking at her underwear. That she hadn't screamed or resisted very much had given him courage. He gazed at her white thighs, desperately trying to stay excited.

A peach. She's a peach. A ripening, juicy peach. I'm going to savour this peach to my heart's content.

Suddenly relaxing her arms and legs, Nanase regained his attention. Then she spoke slowly, enunciating each word carefully.

"I am not a 'ripening peach'. I don't want you 'to savour me to your heart's content'."

In a flash, Katsumi tensed. He was confused. Conflicting thoughts rushed from his subconscious into his consciousness. Doubt began to grow.

What? Why? When did I speak? I didn't say a word.

His mind wandered momentarily, searching for a satisfactory explanation. But this was not an occasion when he could afford to brood over the matter. He grabbed at the first thought that came to mind.

I must have blurted it out unconsciously. I was excited. Lately everyone has been saying that I talk to myself. I did it again – that's all.

Even while Katsumi was convincing himself of this, he was getting more violent so as not to think about it. Actually this behaviour was nothing new to him. Whenever something unpleasant happened that was beyond his comprehension, he would always try to forget it by escaping into his "work".

"No," Nanase shook her head. "You didn't say anything. You didn't 'blurt it out unconsciously'."

Katsumi, who had one arm around her chest and the other around her waist, relaxed his grip ever so slightly. He stared at her wide-eyed.

Nanase grinned and stared back at Katsumi, praying that her intense gaze would unnerve him.

"Stop it," Katsumi spoke for the first time, his voice low and threatening.

It's a mind-reading trick. That's it. It's just some silly mind-reading trick. She's trying to startle me with her guesses. She's hoping I'll get frightened and stop.

"Don't talk nonsense. It's not a 'mind-reading trick'." Nanase shook her head again. "I'm not 'trying to startle you with my guesses'."

It's her mind-reading trick again. Don't be shocked.

Contrary to what he was thinking, however, Katsumi instinctively felt something was wrong. Of its own accord his body separated from Nanase as primitive fear welled up inside him – a fear growing larger by the moment.

Impossible. Impossible. Impossible. Reading people's minds completely. That's crazy. She's a monster. The goblin that knows it all. There is one! It really does exist.

"That's right. I can 'read people's minds completely'," said Nanase as she slowly sat up. "I am the goblin that knows it all."

Katsumi retreated into a corner of the room, still staring at Nanase. His eyes wide and round, he had taken on the expression of an idiot.

The goblin that knows it all. The goblin that knows it all. She's the goblin that knows it all.

The goblin that knows it all was a horror story Katsumi's grandmother had told him as a child. Since the word "telepathy" was not part of Katsumi's vocabulary, it was only natural that this monster would come to mind.

"That's right. Your grandmother told you about the goblin when you were a child," Nanase went on. Acting the part to the hilt, she grinned broadly.

Reason in Katsumi's mind collapsed with a bang.

In his confused consciousness, purpose, will and erotic impulse vanished. All that was left in him was the dread of the unknown and fear of nature common to uncivilized man.

Nanase was no stranger to the legend of the goblin that knows it all. It thrilled her to think that a fear of telepathy had given birth to this legend long ago. Whether the story was Japanese or foreign in origin was of no great consequence. If such telepathists had indeed existed in the past, then it was possible that even today there were many others besides herself.

The goblin that knows it all – referred to in some localities as the mountain man – was a monster who could read people's minds. He lived in the mountains, and was said to have one eye and one leg. He would sometimes go down to a village and approach a man working alone in the fields.

If the villager thought that a creepy-looking fellow had come along, the goblin would immediately say to him: "Just now you looked at me and thought that a creepy-looking fellow had come along." He would then repeat the villager's thoughts one after another. The villager would grow more and more confused, until he could no longer think of anything. The moment his mind became a blank, the monster would pounce on him and eat his brains.

The legend of the mountain man was a bit different. Appearing before a farmer chopping firewood, the mountain man, like the goblin, correctly reads the farmer's thoughts one after another. The farmer is flustered, but he continues chopping. Suddenly a piece of wood flies up and hits the mountain man in his one eye, crushing it. The monster runs off screaming into the mountains, never to return to the village.

Since even the mountain man had been unable to predict the accident, the ending was reassuring in its message that telepathy is not all-powerful. If telepathy had indeed been used as a kind of torture, then this legend offered one passive way to contend with it.

Of course, what really mattered to Nanase was that Katsumi's horror story could be used against him to escape from his clutches. At first she had scared him by revealing her power gradually, but now she realized that this was her only way out.

She understands everything I'm thinking. Don't think. Don't think of anything.

Katsumi, bathed in sweat, sat upright on the tatami mat and stared at Nanase.

"That won't work," Nanase said slowly. "It's impossible for a human being not to think of anything."

"Ah."

Katsumi's chin dropped a few inches. He tried to move, but was paralysed.

She knows everything. Then she might also know about my lusting after Ayako.

"Of course I know. Inside your head, you've undressed Ayako and raped her. Over and over. Over and over."

97

"Yaah."

Katsumi tried to stand up. But he still could not move. His face began to twitch.

"Forgive me. Please forgive me."

Don't think. Keep talking. I mustn't think.

"I'm sorry."

Ayako. I mustn't think.

"I'll never again…"

My daughter-in-law. Don't think. Immoral.

Nanase responded not to Katsumi's words, but only to what appeared in his mind.

"That's right. Even thinking about it is 'immoral'. Raping your daughter-in-law."

Katsumi broke out into a smile. It was a smile coming from the far end of fear and confusion. His consciousness was regressing.

It's Teruko's fault. She's the one to blame. She kept refusing me. Forgive me. Granny. Fairy tales. What's so wrong? Just once in a lifetime… I was level-headed at work. I never fooled around once. All the other section chiefs fooled around with the girls at work. I didn't. After retiring, my free time put all kinds of thoughts into my head.

"That's unfair," said Nanase sharply. "Blaming your wife for your bad conduct. 'Free time after retiring'? You think that kind of excuse will wash with me?"

Katsumi's mind had regressed to his early childhood, into fragments of distant memories.

You're wrong. I'm not to blame. Let's wipe out the bad guys. I'm the little peach boy Momotaro. I'll teach them a lesson. I'll go and teach them a lesson. I'm not the one who has to be taught a lesson. OK. Granny, let's go teach the bad guys a lesson.

"No, You're the one who has to be taught a lesson. I'm going to teach you a lesson."

Nanase had no idea where this meaningless exchange would lead them. Still, once begun, she felt compelled to see it through to the end.

"Ugh…"

Katsumi stood up finally and stumbled into the hallway.

I'm leaving. I'm leaving. Granny. I'm going to Granny's. I'm going to Granny's.

"Wait!" Nanase hurriedly followed him, throwing on the pyjamas Katsumi had ripped off her. "I'm not going to let you leave."

Katsumi was about to sit down in the hall, but with Nanase's voice raining down on him from behind, he stumbled off again. He began to crawl up the dark stairs.

I've got to go back. I've got to go back. Go back to Granny's.

Nanase stood at the bottom of the stairs, watching a grotesque Katsumi squirm idiotically in the darkness.

Any further punishment would be too cruel. But Nanase could not stop now. Once Katsumi regained his reason, his existence would be a terrible threat to her. He would know about her ESP, and there was no telling what he might do. He could blab about it to anyone.

Even if no one believed him, he would be the only person in the world who knew about her power. For that reason alone she had to do whatever was necessary to obliterate his existence.

In order to protect herself, Nanase had no choice but to destroy his mind.

She faced the dark second-floor landing and shouted, "Your grandmother isn't there. She isn't anywhere. That grandmother of yours who was always sitting in the upstairs parlour – she's dead. She's been dead for ages. Dead. Dead. The granny who protected you from everything is gone. There's no place for you to go to."

All the decorations fell gently from the roof of Katsumi's consciousness, and in a flash the room turned into a void. In that instant, his consciousness became so perfectly empty that it took Nanase's breath away. Katsumi stood up on the landing and, just as Nanase wondered whether his mind had really become a blank, he started to laugh quietly to himself.

"Hee hee hee."

The strange clutter inside Katsumi's subconscious broke down its last restraining barrier and all at once burst forth onto the surface. Katsumi had gone mad.

"Ha ha ha."

"Oh." Nanase covered her face and cowered. She had never glimpsed the mind of a madman before. The muddle of Katsumi's id, full of a fright far more primitive than the most irrational of fears, now gave

100

rise to a coarse, devilish laughter that came swooping down the stairs and over Nanase's head.

In a panic, Nanase let down the latch in her own mind, shutting Katsumi's mind out. But the horror would not leave her.

She could not stop shaking.

Finally Nanase stood up slowly and stared at Katsumi.

Her victim was there, laughing senselessly. She had accomplished her purpose.

From the dark staircase into the dark hallway, throughout the darkened house, the mad Katsumi's laughter spread.

"What's wrong? What are you laughing at?" Teruko's footsteps came pattering down the hallway.

"Nana, what's happened? Where are you? What are you laughing at?"

5

The Saint in the
Flames of Hell

"The Negishis? Dear, isn't Mrs Negishi that quiet, refined woman?"

"Yes, I think so."

Nanase had asked the couple who ran the stationery store by the station for directions to the Negishi residence. In a town that did not seem particularly small, Mrs Negishi's refinement must have quite outshone that of the other housewives – enough to have created an impression even at the local stationery store.

The Negishis lived in a modern neighbourhood about five minutes uphill from the station. Unlike the other houses with their spacious, American-style front lawns, the Negishi residence was built on a stone-faced embankment, surrounded by high concrete walls.

The intelligent-looking Mrs Negishi led Nanase into a living room that faced a large garden, and, without being overly inquisitive, chatted about this and that. Nanase had heard about her from her previous employer and, as she had pictured her, Mrs Negishi was a woman of elegant speech and bearing, with a gentle expression.

"I have a baby," she said. She was smiling, but her eyes were not. "A ten-month-old boy, so I have a lot

105

on my hands. Since my husband often works at home, I have to look after him as well. That's why I've asked you to come."

It was obvious from her way of speaking that she feared the world would think ill of a twenty-nine-year-old housewife hiring a maid. She was trying to justify herself.

However, her near-perfect act could not fool Nanase's telepathy. After ten minutes of conversation, Nanase realized that Mrs Negishi's modesty, refinement and cordiality were all a charade. Any modesty and refinement that could impress the couple who ran the local stationery store were probably only achieved with a bit of overacting.

In their three years of marriage, Mrs Negishi had been playing a role before her husband as well. For her, the only way to keep her marriage going was either to maintain a tight control over her husband or to continue her charade. Since she considered herself an intellectual, she chose the latter course.

Kikuko Negishi's husband, Shinzo, was an associate professor at a private university and, like his wife, was twenty-nine years old. They had fallen in love when they were both psychology students. In fact, Shinzo's specialization in psychology was one of the reasons that Nanase had decided to take this job.

That day, Shinzo returned at four in the afternoon when his lecture was over. His tiny eyes peered from behind rimless glasses and his expression was almost always the same. When Kikuko introduced Nanase in the living room, his mouth suddenly tensed.

Nanase Hita. Hita. Hita. I've heard that name before.

Hita was an unusual last name, and it had sparked Shinzo's memory. Nanase tried to explore his consciousness, but all she could find there was that the name seemed to belong to someone connected with his research. Shinzo himself was unable to recall who it was, and he immediately started thinking about something else.

"Don't go into my study," he told Nanase. "I'll tell you when I want it cleaned."

The academic-minded Shinzo would never put up with a cloddish girl straightening out the papers on his desk or rearranging the books on his shelves.

"But if I leave his study the way it is, the dust piles up," Kikuko said to Nanase with a smile after Shinzo went off to his study. "Insects breed and it's not sanitary. So sometimes I clean it without telling him. If he finds out, he gets angry. Still…"

Kikuko was using cleanliness and order as a weapon. She knew that Shinzo could never brand her a bad wife just for cleaning his study; at the same time she wanted to show the world what an absent-minded and childish scholar her husband was. If word of her problems with this temperamental husband of hers got around, then her wifely act would be all the more convincing. In Kikuko's logic, the role of "good wife" could only be carried off by turning her husband into a clown.

As Nanase saw it, on a deeper level, Kikuko deliberately wanted to belittle her husband's scholarship; she couldn't ridicule Shinzo without making fun of his work as well. Yet, vain as she was, she would pray fervently for her husband's academic success. Kikuko herself remained completely unaware of this contradiction inside her.

"You don't have to worry. I won't make you do it," said Kikuko, still smiling. She had misinterpreted Nanase's pensive look. "I'll do the cleaning myself. I'm used to getting yelled at." She wanted Nanase to like her.

She should feel sorry for me and blab to everyone about Shinzo's odd ways.

Kikuko was still thinking this as she fed her baby, who had woken up and started to fuss.

But she may not work out – she seems the quiet type.

Nanase was surprised to discover that here was the real reason Kikuko had hired her. In fact, the following day Kikuko began her machinations to make sure Nanase would notice her husband's peculiar, childish ways. He'd extinguish his cigarettes in teacups or bowls; when he finished eating, he'd stick his chopsticks into the rice remaining in his bowl; left to himself, he'd use the same handkerchief every day, and after wiping his desk and shoes with it, he'd wipe his hands and face, and so on. Actually, from Nanase's viewpoint, these eccentricities were only indications of the indifferent, simple nature of men.

Obviously, Kikuko herself could not blab about her husband. If it became clear that she was bad-mouthing him, she'd no longer be the good wife.

When Shinzo was home, he'd spend almost all of the time in the study and appear only at mealtimes. When he occasionally ran into Nanase, he would try to recall the person he knew named Hita. Always the face refused to surface, and his thoughts would immediately turn elsewhere. These thoughts often concerned his mistress, Akiko, who was a student in the psychology department.

The sofa in my office, late at night. The cold bed in the inn. Her cold flesh. No one knows. It's nothing but a cheap affair. I'm already tired of her. There are other possibilities. I'm better off breaking up with Akiko before anyone finds out about it.

However, it wasn't likely that someone so indifferent in his approach to appearance could carry off an affair unnoticed. First of all, Kikuko could sense it. She didn't know the name of the woman, but traces she found on his handkerchiefs convinced her she was right.

There are lots of girls studying psychology. Even a man like Shinzo can find someone who would sleep with him.

Kikuko had even guessed that he was sleeping with a girl, but that he'd have no trouble moving on to someone new. Even granting that she knew the atmosphere at school, for someone without telepathic powers her insight was amazing.

"What time will you be home today?" Kikuko always asked her husband at breakfast on the days he went to the university. Shinzo usually gave some mechanical reply. It never occurred to him that Kikuko would actually remember the time. That she might prepare a meal to coincide with his return was beyond his comprehension. For him, eating was something virtually forced on him when he happened to be at home during mealtimes. Shinzo had no interest in food, and Nanase found his primitive taste buds a source of wonder.

His lecture ended at 3.50. It's now 7.40. Three hours for sex. He'll be home soon.

Kikuko, who could figure out exactly when her husband was engaging in sex, would spend the same time burning with jealousy, hugging her baby to herself and brooding. Kikuko had no outlet for her violent jealousy. Whenever Nanase would peer into her mind and see this hell, she'd hastily retract her telepathic antennae and let down the latch on her own consciousness.

Her husband's affair was the one thing Kikuko kept hidden from Nanase. She wanted to maintain an intellectual superiority over Shinzo. If his adultery became common knowledge, people would be bound to blame her as well.

"You must have had an exhausting day, coming home so late."

When he'd return after his sexual dalliance, while sharing a late meal, Kikuko would hurl this at him

110

spitefully. She would smile at him sympathetically. But sarcasm was wasted on Shizo.

"The young professors are made to do all the work for the conference. I don't have any time for my own research."

Tonight Akiko was unusually passionate. Maybe she can tell I'm losing interest and is trying to stave off the break-up.

He's thinking about her. He's remembering their love-making. He's thinking about it while he's eating. That face. What does he look like when they're?... What kind of a girl is she? What does he say to her? No doubt the same things he used to say to me. I'm sure she likes to gossip. I wonder if she's told anyone. She must have another boyfriend, so maybe she's told him.

Akiko wouldn't tell anyone, would she? I think she's sleeping with a student as well. She's always talking to him. The same guy. Dangerous. Tamako doesn't have a boyfriend. Tamako's safer.

Even when he works, he can't get his mind off her. That's why he spends so much time shut up in his study. And that's why his research hasn't got very far, if you think about all the time he's put into it. Otherwise by now he'd be... And his research isn't so difficult. Just when will he get to be a full professor?

As she had often done in her previous jobs, Nanase avoided eating with the family as much as possible. She had to make an enormous effort to eat without reacting to the endless stream of meanness in the minds of the couple.

She couldn't, however, let down her latch and completely shut out their thoughts. She had to find out the identity of the Hita in Shinzo's memory. Considering that Shinzo's field of study was psychology, she couldn't underestimate the danger.

Shinzo rarely dwelt on his highly theoretical research during meals. Since he could only make deductions after examining a wide assortment of data, he almost never came up with an idea of importance while eating. As a result, Nanase had virtually no chance to gather fresh information about her powers, assuming there was any, from Shinzo's mind. And since she wasn't allowed to clean his study, her hopes of secretly reading his books had been dashed. In due course she'd find a way to get into his study, but it seemed wiser to wait for the opportunity to present itself rather than do something rash that might arouse unnecessary suspicion.

One day, when Shinzo came home late because he really had been preparing for a conference, Kikuko was unable to figure out whether or not he was telling the truth. She was still bothered about it during dinner, and she observed her husband closely.

Which was it? Was he really working? Or was he having sex?

Late that night, when Nanase went to the bathroom, she noticed a light on by the sink. Peering from the corner of the hallway, she saw the tall, thin Kikuko in a stark white nightgown standing in front of the mirror. She was holding a condom by her fingertips, staring at her husband's semen. She seemed to be measuring the amount with her eyes. Kikuko had a pale complexion, sharply etched features and big eyes. These eyes were framed in black and opened so wide Nanase could make out Kikuko's dilated pupils. Nanase shuddered at the ghastly sight and quietly returned to her room.

As the days passed, Kikuko's jealousy developed into a fixation. Paradoxically, her play-acting was approaching perfection. While Nanase realized that Kikuko was unconsciously protecting herself from an eruption of her emotions, she also knew that this could have the adverse effect of precipitating a mental collapse. If Kikuko would only bring her jealousy to the surface, accuse her husband, clutch at him and cry hysterically, then she would feel better, thought Nanase. Of course she also knew that Kikuko was quite incapable of such behaviour.

Shinzo, completely unaware of Kikuko's inner agony, took advantage of the fact that his wife didn't seem to suspect anything and began an affair with Tamako. Now he made only half-hearted efforts to hide the evidence that would have worried him more in the past. For over a year he had been disgusted by Kikuko, who'd act like a painted harlot to add spice to their nightly bedroom scenes. He had even tired of sex with Akiko. The egotistical scholar, he was only interested in three things: his status at the university, his research and his sex life. Even worse, he didn't feel the least trace of guilt. After all the self-denials of his student days, he seemed to think that it was now his God-given right to do whatever he pleased. And becoming a professor so young had made him arrogant and self-centred. He had lost all sense of common morals!

Nanase was finding it more and more unbearable to join them at the dinner table.

He's seeing a new woman.

I prefer Tamako. Kikuko's such a fool with the way she acts. She thinks she can keep me chained to her.

Just once I'd like to spread out on the bed his lipstick-stained shirt. Maybe I'll do it. I wonder if I should tell him I've known for ages. What would he do then? He'd deny it. No. He's too childish and selfish. He'd get upset. He'd take it out on me. And refuse to have sex with me.

Tamako is more genuine than Akiko. She has no affectations. She doesn't act, she keeps nothing back.

The end of us. The end of our marriage. But it wouldn't come to divorce. His status. His position at school. Any scandal in his private life would affect his advancement. He's calculating. He's calculating. Calculating.

The bitch. Pretending to be a good wife and mother – acting so ladylike and refined. For all that, treating me like a child. She has no idea of the importance of my research. For all her modesty, she lives only for sex.

Young girls these days have no qualms. About stealing someone's husband. The impudence.

Anger towards the unknown woman burned like a red flame in Kikuko's mind, and for a moment the hand holding her chopsticks shook violently. But she immediately put on a smile, turned to her husband and asked him sweetly if he wanted any more soup.

I'll kill him.

"OK."

What's with that tone of voice?

"Nana, would you please reheat the soup?"

I really feel like killing him.

"Here you are."

It wouldn't come to divorce. Once he's found out, he'd just fool around more openly. He'd be parading his affairs in front of me.

She just lives for sex. She demanded it last night. She'll demand it again tonight. Her smell gives me a headache. Makes me sick. How can she consider herself an intellectual? Dried-up old bag.

I'll kill him in the act. Both of them. It'll be the ruin of all of us. Newspapers. Tabloids. Murderess Lurks Behind Gentle Façade. Big headlines.

Tamako's youthful sex. Young muscles, young legs, young behind. To give my love only to this woman. Obviously I was made for better things than that.

Just my luck to start working here when they're having their first marital crisis, thought Nanase. What rotten timing.

Two months after Nanase had arrived at the house, Kikuko went to her parents' for the day to show them their grandson.

That afternoon Shinzo went off to the university, and Nanase was left alone. She quickly took care of the cleaning and washing, and then, with her heart pounding, she sneaked into Shinzo's study.

The Western-style room was about seventy square feet. Bookshelves extended from floor to ceiling on all four walls, interrupted only by the door and windows. Almost all of the books were on psychology. There were more books piled up on the parquet floor and on a large desk facing the window that looked out into the back garden. Ten or so volumes lay open. Yet, strangely enough, there was no sense of disorder; even Nanase, who knew little about the academic world, could tell right away that everything was carefully organized.

More than half the books were Western, and most of these seemed to be in German. Many of the newer books were written in English and placed on one part of a bookshelf; among these were the parapsychology studies by Rhine and Saul that Nanase herself had read. Her heart skipped a beat. She couldn't read German, so she removed a few recent English volumes near Rhine's book and tried skimming through them, frustrated by her meagre high-school ability. She finally figured out that two of the books were experimental reports on ESP.

Shinzo must have done research on parapsychology! He had written comments in the margins of the books and had underlined certain parts in red. And in the shelves filled with recent publications, there were some popular books on parapsychology written by Japanese authors.

Although one glance at the books and materials spread out on the desk made it clear that Shinzo's current research was unrelated to parapsychology, Nanase was unable to shake off her anxiety.

Looking further, Nanase discovered a thick file labelled "Psi Ability" on a shelf full of files and folders. She opened it excitedly. Psi ability, she knew, referred to ESP.

The ESP ability of about one hundred people, apparently chosen at random, had been measured through tests and recorded on cards resembling medical charts. Judging from the dates, it was clear that Shinzo had been involved in ESP research while still a student.

From among the cards, Nanase discovered one with her father's name.

Seiichiro Hita.

Nanase was stunned.

Even if Shinzo couldn't remember exactly who her father was, the fact that he could still remember the name of one out of a hundred subjects must mean that her father had shown some singular ability. The card was a mishmash of numbers and symbols completely indecipherable to Nanase, but instinctively she sensed danger – for herself.

Just at that moment, as if to add fuel to Nanase's anxiety, the living-room telephone rang.

Nanase panicked. If she left the card where it was and Shinzo came home while she was still answering the phone, she might never get another chance to go into his study. Nanase removed the card and quickly returned the book to its place on the shelf.

It was Kikuko on the phone. After asking if Shinzo was home, she said that she'd be late and gave Nanase detailed instructions for dinner. Nanase was unable to read Kikuko's mind over the phone, but if her husband hadn't returned yet, Kikuko probably just assumed he was engaged in, as she put it, one of his "beastly interludes". In which case she could stay out later herself.

After she hung up the telephone, Nanase stared blankly at the card in her hand. Oh no, she thought. Not having time to open the clasp of the file, she had ripped the card out and torn it in the corner. Now it would be impossible to put the card back.

If Shinzo remembered who Nanase's father was and discovered that the card was missing, then he'd suspect Nanase first. He might start checking into her background, wondering what she had to hide. And yet there was even greater danger in returning the torn card. On some completely unrelated occasion, he might find that the card had once been ripped out of the file.

Once Shinzo suspects me and begins to investigate, he might uncover my power, thought Nanase with a shiver. She could not keep still. What a blunder I've committed, she thought, stamping her feet in vexation. The worst possible scenarios of what might happen to her – scenes she had imagined over and over in the past – flooded her mind. Placed on a laboratory table, surrounded by scholars, cross-examined, her face made public, an object of contempt... Ever since Nanase had realized that the disclosure of her power would spell her doom, these frightening images had tormented her. Her teeth chattered in terror.

As she saw it, the fate of a heretic was the same no matter what the age. After being loathed and feared by all "normal" people, what would be waiting for her? Surely not the death sentence, but there would be experimentation, public exhibition and ostracism, and for Nanase this was more frightening than a death sentence. Yet she could predict all of this with some accuracy. Realistically speaking, once human society learnt she had superhuman powers, it would never leave her alone.

In a daze, Nanase wandered aimlessly from room to room. Just when her thoughts ran to burning the card in her hands, the front doorbell rang. Nanase realized that Shinzo was standing on the porch.

He's come home early.

Nanase panicked, folded the card in half, hid it behind a beam in the corner of the guest room and dashed to the front door. As she ran, she rubbed her cheeks with both hands: the colour must have drained from her face.

When she opened the door, Shinzo stared sharply at her. On reading Shinzo's mind, Nanase let out a silent scream. He had remembered who Seiichiro Hita was.

She's his daughter. I'll test her at once. Is psi ability hereditary?

His test results should be in my file. I'll go get them.

"Wasn't your father the Mr Hita who headed the general-affairs department at Takebe Paper Manufacturing?" asked Shinzo as he took off his shoes.

"Yes, that's right." Nanase answered resignedly, knowing that Shinzo had already checked into her background. Trying to deceive him now would be even more dangerous.

"I want to talk to you." He stared at her again. "Would you like to come to my study?"

Nanase knew it was hopeless, but she hesitated a bit, and then answered, "Mrs Negishi told me to go shopping for dinner."

"Don't worry about that." Shinzo frowned.

I'm the head of this house.

"It's important. Come right now," he ordered.

Kikuko's got even the maid to treat me like a fool.

Nanase nodded, realizing there was no way to get out of it.

"All right. Then I'll bring some tea right away."

Shinzo grunted and went straight to his study without bothering to change.

Nanase removed the card from the beam, so she could at least destroy the evidence that she had taken

120

it. She burned it over the kitchen stove. Should I pack my bags and escape right now? No, that would be a mistake – I'd attract even more attention and would be found out in the end anyway. I'll decide what to do after I figure out how much Shinzo knows.

When Nanase, bearing a tea tray, walked into the study, she imagined that this was how a suspect in a criminal case feels on entering the interrogation room of police headquarters. As she had expected, Shinzo had taken down the file in question and was searching through the cards, puzzled.

That's funny. It's the only card missing. I wonder if I gave it to Professor Kabashima because of the unusual results. Even so, I would have kept a copy.

Professor Kabashima had been Shinzo's adviser when he was a student. He had been especially interested in parapsychology, but luckily for Nanase he had died five years earlier. Nanase was somewhat relieved to find that Shinzo didn't seem to be linking the disappearance of the card to her. She waited for him to speak, while painstakingly reading every single thought in his consciousness.

"Sit down here." Shinzo pointed to a small stool next to his steel desk chair. He started questioning her immediately. "Is your father well?"

Why is the only daughter of the general-affairs manager of Takebe Paper Manufacturing working as a maid?

"He's dead," Nanase answered. Shinzo had asked the question, knowing her father was dead, so he could

gauge Nanase's reaction. She spoke without expression.
"He died two years ago, the year before I graduated
from high school."

"I'm so sorry."

I've got to find that card.

"Did you know my father?" Nanase decided to take
the initiative and pick his brain on various matters
without giving him a chance to ask questions.

"Yes, I do. I did, rather. I remembered today at the
university." Shinzo had been talking to an old classmate
at the university when he recalled who Seiichiro
Hita was, and he had called up Nanase's reference to
confirm her father's name. "Your father once helped
with some research. This is probably difficult for you
to understand, but he took part in a psychological
experiment known as an ESP test."

*His results were amazing. Kabashima was surprised,
too. That's why his name stuck in my mind.*

I was right after all, thought Nanase as she immediately considered her next question. Whatever
else, she had to keep Shinzo from asking why she was
working as a live-in maid. That she feared her power
might be detected if she stayed in one place for too long
was something even wild horses could not drag out of
her.

"Uh... when was that?"

"Seven years ago."

*Why does she keep pestering me with questions? I can't
ask her anything. It should be the other way around.*

Nanase read in Shinzo's mind that at the time the Takebe Paper Manufacturing building had been located next to the psychology department and that they had looked for subjects among the company's employees. Her father had probably taken the test for fun. Little could he have imagined what disaster this would bring to his only daughter.

Shinzo was itching to give Nanase the ESP test. If she asked him any more questions, the egocentricity common to scholars would come to the surface and he'd flare up at her.

"Your father had a special ability." Now that Nanase had lapsed into silence, Shinzo started explaining. "Everyone was surprised. We wanted to give him further tests, but seeing that he was general-affairs manager and busy with his work, the opportunity never presented itself. And after a while, we forgot about it." Actually, the experiment had been discontinued due to Professor Kabashima's sudden death. "However, it really is a shame that Mr Hita died. Did you hear anything about this experiment from your father?"

"No, I didn't." This was the truth.

Nanase knew better than anyone, of course, that her father hadn't been a telepathist. Considering the extent of her own power, however, he probably did have some kind of ESP ability. But even if he had been told the results of the experiment, her practical-minded father would probably have laughed it off without a second thought. At the time Nanase was already in junior high school and obsessed with her own power, so she would have remembered if her father had mentioned the test.

"This is probably difficult for you to understand, but these are ESP cards," said Shinzo, taking up the cards he had laid out on his desk and showing them to Nanase.

"This is probably difficult for you to understand" seemed to be one of Shinzo's stock phrases. But Nanase, of course, was well aware of what ESP cards were. They resembled playing cards, with five cards each of five symbols – a cross, a star, a circle, a square and a wave – making a total of twenty-five cards in a set.

"Professor Rhine from Duke University made these cards for his experiments. Now this is how we conduct the test. The tester and testee sit facing each other with a screen between them. Each time the tester turns up a card, the testee guesses the pattern. In other words, this experiment measures what's known as clairvoyance, one kind of extrasensory perception. Your father did extraordinarily well on this test. If he had guessed correctly only by coincidence, the probability would have been less than one out of ten to the tenth power, an amazing result. In other words, we can safely say that his rate of success was absolutely beyond coincidence. Are you following me?"

Don't make me repeat myself, it's a waste of time. Tell me you understand.

Of course Nanase understood only too well. But with great effort she tried to look stupid. "Uh, well… sort of…"

Moron. Her father was smarter.

Shinzo continued explaining, his annoyance increasing. "In short, I want you to take the same test. It's clear that your father had a special ability. So I'm thinking that you might have inherited his ESP, his extrasensory perception. How about it?" Shinzo asked her in as light a manner as possible, and yet in a tone that would have made it impossible to refuse. "Will you give it a try?"

"Uh…" Nanase fidgeted. "Now?"

"Uh, yes." Shinzo wavered for a moment. He realized he lacked the witness necessary for the experiment. But he told himself that if the results were good, he could then have her officially tested at the university. "That's right. Now, if possible."

"Well…" Nanase's voice faltered. "I have to prepare dinner before the mistress gets back. I'll be in trouble if I don't. She'll be home soon."

Shinzo's eyes burned in anger.

Idiot. The girl's an idiot.

He had always looked down on uneducated people for being unable to understand his research, and the fact that Nanase was using his wife as an excuse made him resent the girl even more.

"I told you that didn't matter, didn't I?"

It occurred to Nanase that playing the dull-witted girl might be to her benefit. If Shinzo thought that she couldn't possibly have ESP, he might give up the experiment. But Nanase also knew that Shinzo would never give up so easily. Inside his mind, she could see ambition, self-interest and a lust for fame.

Shinzo himself was more interested in the research he was currently tackling than in parapsychology, but he was thinking that if Nanase did prove to have ESP, he could publish new discoveries on its hereditary nature, and at the same time present the unpublished results of the late Professor Kabashima's work as his own. It was even conceivable that the mass media might pick up on the sensational nature of his research. He realized, of course, that the Japanese academic world still made light of parapsychology, and this might pose a problem. But in America and the Soviet Union, universities with parapsychological research centres were not uncommon, and so if all else failed, he could hope for a warm critical reception abroad.

Nanase was determined to avoid an ESP test at all costs. She did not know if she had clairvoyant powers or not. Since she would inadvertently read her opponent's mind, she had always avoided playing cards and similar types of games. But even if she deliberately chose wrong answers, she'd have no idea what kind of unexpected evaluation might be formed – there was even a danger in making too many mistakes. Nanase knew of an actual case where a testee had made so many errors that the results were carefully gone over, and it was discovered that cards removed had been guessed correctly one after another. If Nanase had clairvoyant powers, then there was a great risk that in trying to avoid the right answers which would appear in Shinzo's mind, she might unconsciously correctly guess the order of the cards from another place in the series.

Taking advantage of Shinzo's all-too-apparent anger, Nanase put on an even blanker expression, placed her clenched fists on her knees, deliberately avoided looking at Shinzo and spoke in a plainly obstinate tone.

"I don't want to take any psychological test."

Inside Shinzo a desire to scream battled it out with his self-control.

The moronic girl. Don't get angry. Isn't this the response ordinary people always have towards psychology? Damn Kikuko. Just what kind of idiotic notions about my work did she fill the maid's head with?

Keeping his emotions in check, he started talking to Nanase in what was for him a highly considerate manner. "Psychology isn't the frightening science you think it is. I'm not going to be able to understand everything you're thinking or hypnotize you or anything like that. What I meant by an experiment..."

For almost an hour he tried persuading her. Suppressing his emotions, Shinzo gently admonished her for accepting these misconceptions about psychology, brought up how intelligent her father was, and in the end even hinted that he'd pay her a fee.

Occasionally there would be a small emotional explosion: "Don't you understand yet?" "How can I get through to you?"

But he'd immediately regain his calm and forge on with his appeal. The kinder he was, however, the more dubious Nanase looked, and the angrier he got, the more she pouted stubbornly. And she doggedly kept her silence.

Where does this ignorance and obstinacy come from? Such a non-human, animal-like girl is better off dead. She won't talk any more. Damn her, she's shut up like a clam.

Why do I have to suffer so, why do I have to take such horrible insults lying down, thought Nanase, suddenly breaking into tears in spite of herself. She started weeping uncontrollably.

Nanase's tears were more than Shinzo could put up with. *Tears of an ignoramus. Tears of a pig. I've had enough. Is it that awful? Then go do what you like.*

"You idiot. All right. Just leave," he screamed at her, no longer trying to hide his repugnance. Then he turned his back on Nanase, angry and frustrated. He hadn't given up, however. He was already thinking of how to get another chance at her.

When Nanase left the study, sobbing, Shinzo's fingertips were tapping the desk convulsively. She couldn't stop crying. Her tears kept welling up. For the first time in her life, Nanase cursed her power from the bottom of her heart.

Nanase was still crying in the living room when she sensed nearby a consciousness churning violently like a storm. She looked up in surprise. It was Kikuko. When had she come home? She was standing upright, staring at Nanase with a look of shock on her pale face.

Even the maid! He's even gone after the maid. Even the maid.

"You're wrong," Nanase almost screamed out, then quickly held her tongue. What a horrible misunderstanding.

"Oh, you're back," she said instead, hurriedly wiping away her tears. She put on a normal face and tried speaking calmly, but she couldn't hide the trembling in her voice.

Kikuko was now sure that Shinzo had "gone after" Nanase. A fire burned inside her with a force never seen before.

The beast! The beast!

Once she was fully convinced of this, however, her elegant smile and gentle look returned.

"What's wrong?"

She came up to Nanase anxiously, putting on an expression of benevolence befitting a saint. "Why are you crying?" she asked in a voice brimming with concern.

She's been raped. She's been raped. He raped her. She's been raped by him.

"It's nothing."

"Oh." Kikuko decided that it wouldn't look right if she pressed the girl too much.

129

The wrathful fire burning in Kikuko reminded Nanase of the red blaze from a crematorium that she had seen when she was a little girl. Or perhaps she was recalling a tableau from a "Heaven and Hell" peep show at a temple festival she had gone to in her childhood. Then again, she might never have had such memories. Overwhelmed by the force of this violent, primitive anger, she had mistaken it for a memory, experiencing a sort of déjà vu.

To think that one human being could abhor another so much. The image was driving Nanase insane, and yet she could not take her eyes off it. She could only quake in fear at this explosion of primal anger.

I can't work here any longer, thought Nanase. But she had to keep Shinzo from seeking her out. The only way to stop him was to present him with a crisis so enormous that it would make him forget her completely. In which case, she had no choice but to make use of Kikuko's explosive anger.

Nanase let down her latch to shut out Kikuko's consciousness. She had to prepare herself mentally by blocking out her furious thoughts. She sidled up to her and began, "Mrs Negishi, there's something I want to say to you."

Kikuko smiled calmly at Nanase while cradling her fretting baby. "What is it?"

"The other day on my day off, I went to see a movie. And on my way back, I saw him." All the while avoiding Kikuko's gaze, she spoke in one breath. "Mr Negishi was leaving a hotel with a woman."

If Kikuko asked, Nanase was prepared to tell her the name of the hotel and time: she had read it in Shinzo's mind. But Kikuko remained silent, her expression unchanging. Instead, her baby burst out crying. Kikuko seemed to have squeezed him extra hard.

Nanase went on. "Once before I saw Mr Negishi with a woman in a coffee shop. I was already inside, but your husband didn't notice me and sat down in the booth right behind me. Mr Negishi and this woman seemed to be... you know... I could tell by their talk." Nanase stared straight at Kikuko. "That's all."

"Thank you." Kikuko stared back at Nanase while rocking the baby, still maintaining her gentle smile. "But don't tell anyone else about this." She had clearly resolved to play the role of faithful wife who endured her husband's debaucheries.

"You are sure, Mrs Negishi?" Nanase urged Kikuko on. "Your husband's having an affair!"

"I understand how you feel." Once again, Kikuko knitted her brow in concern. "My husband did do something to you after all."

Kikuko was probably thinking that Nanase was telling on him because she felt sorry for her fellow victim. But Nanase didn't make any reply. The longer she kept silent, the more furious Kikuko was likely to become.

"No," Nanase finally denied weakly. "I'm all right."

"I'm relieved to hear that."

Nanase looked at Kikuko's staring eyes. For whatever reason, huge teardrops welled up and came streaking down her cheeks.

While Kikuko kept on smiling, the tears flowed from her unblinking eyes. The weirdness of this was beyond description. Obviously they weren't tears of relief.

Kikuko must now be firmly convinced that her husband had raped Nanase, but Nanase knew that she would never confirm it by asking him. And he wasn't likely to tell his wife of his own accord about the ESP test; he knew she'd only ridicule it.

Suddenly Kikuko turned away, wiped her cheeks with the back of her hands, and casually asked Nanase the following question.

"What did my husband talk about with the woman he met in the coffee shop?"

"Both of them were bad-mouthing you," Nanase answered. "They were making fun of you."

All at once the latch in Nanase's consciousness sprung open as angry waves came bursting into her thoughts.

"Ohh…" Nanase collapsed onto the linoleum floor. Kikuko's violent anger had taken hold of not only Nanase's mind but of her very body as well.

When she looked up, she saw Kikuko, the baby in her arms, consumed by a raging fire. Kikuko was standing erect in the centre of the blaze, still smiling benevolently, but with her eyes opened wide as she looked down at Nanase. In her anger she chanted sutras, whether consciously or unconsciously. The force and horror of her will made it impossible for Nanase to cut her fury off from her mind. All she could do was shake.

"Pl-Please…" Nanase screamed out hoarsely. "I want to leave."

"Of course you do." Licked by the flames, the virtuous woman had already lost interest in the girl. She smiled at her as she said goodbye.

Early the next morning Nanase left the Negishis.

Two days later Nanase read in the newspaper that Mrs Negishi had killed her baby and then committed suicide in the bath. It was not likely that Shinzo Negishi would ever try to find Nanase.

6

*The Grass Is
Greener*

"Starting tomorrow, would you mind helping out the Ichikawas next door for a week?" Teruo Takagi asked Nanase. "Mr Ichikawa is working at home now."

"It's fine with me, but..." Nanase answered.

Teruo, who had a stubby neck and thick lips, frowned. "I've already spoken to Naoko."

Then he returned to the medical report on his lap.

During the month Nanase had been working at the Takagis', she had never once seen Teruo read a medical textbook while relaxing in the study-living room. He would either be leafing through thin reports or the newspaper. Otherwise he'd be watching foreign movies on TV. And yet Teruo was a doctor who ran a small clinic on the first floor of the apartment building.

Even though he was only forty, Nanase could tell that he had already lost interest in his work.

There were lots of medical texts lining the bookshelves, but Nanase wasn't fooled. When she peered into Teruo's mind, she found him preoccupied with his position inside the medical academy, the one and only interest he showed towards his job. His concern for his patients amounted to a momentary thought for a particularly troubling case. Needless to say, he hated emergency house calls.

Naoko came home. She had gone to have an autumn suit tailored at her favourite boutique. Since she never told her husband her plans, he had no idea where she had been.

Without a word, Naoko went into her bedroom to change. Teruo didn't say anything either. He'd only come out with something sarcastic and then his wife would lash back with even more bitter sarcasm. Naoko treated him with contempt. But what Teruo didn't understand was the real reason behind this contempt.

Since they lived in a three-bedroom apartment, Nanase was able to tune into their minds freely no matter what room they were in. While Naoko was changing in the bedroom, she was thinking of her next-door neighbour, Shogo Ichikawa. They had just exchanged nods at the entrance. At thirty-seven, he was the same age as herself. Shogo was an architectural designer specializing in stores and, unlike Teruo, was neither fat nor lazy. The reason Naoko, in spite of her age, blushed every time she met Shogo was because all his good qualities were lacking in her husband.

"I spoke to Nana," Teruo said to Naoko when she came into the living room. "She says she won't mind going."

The nerve of ordering me to take care of such chores.

"Oh." Naoko spoke without turning to face Nanase. "Do your best, Nana."

"Whatever you say." To gauge Naoko's feelings, Nanase deliberately spoke slowly, hinting at some double meaning.

138

As she predicted, Naoko turned to look at her, startled. By peering into Naoko's consciousness at that instant, Nanase learnt that she genuinely wanted her to help out at the Ichikawas'. Naoko was hoping that this would give her the opportunity to meet Shogo.

"Go inform the Ichikawas." Teruo stared fixedly at Naoko.

He could tell that his wife was interested in their next-door neighbour. In the past she would always praise Mr Ichikawa for the way he did his work, but now she never said anything, a clear indication that her interest in him had taken on a new dimension. So to test his wife's reaction, he had deliberately spoken with an unmerited gravity, in the imperious tone his wife detested.

"You don't have to tell me that." Picking up on what her husband was intimating, Naoko showed her anger.

Why don't I just tell him I'd be delighted to go right now? Shogo's not home. I should go later.

"I'll go later." Then she added by way of a retaliation, "Mr Ichikawa isn't home now."

Teruo tried to curve his lips into a smile, but ended up with quite a different expression. He knew that inside him lay a fragment of feeling approximating jealousy, and he was mulling this over unpleasantly.

"There's no point in speaking to Mrs Ichikawa." Naoko continued her attack as she watched her husband's face twitch. Her remark was an indirect cut at Teruo for leaving all the bothersome matters to her.

Hearing this, Teruo was finally able to manage a bitter smile.

Next door, the husband makes all the important decisions. But in my household, this pushy woman...

For Nanase's benefit, Naoko decided to say something nice about Mrs Ichikawa. "Mrs Ichikawa is so soft-spoken, isn't she?" Then, realizing she had come out with the same sarcasm Teruo would have directed at her, Naoko quickly disappeared into the kitchen.

Maybe Naoko's figured out how I feel about Mrs Ichikawa, Teruo thought nervously. However, he immediately concluded that there was nothing to worry about, and then deliberately shouted his agreement into the kitchen. "She really is."

Once more Teruo's eyes fell on his report, but his mind was taken up with the petite, attractive woman next door. Compared to the large-framed, strong-willed Naoko, Mrs Ichikawa seemed much more feminine. He had examined her a number of times, and each time had been attracted to her white skin and shapely breasts. Perhaps she had sensed how he felt, for lately she'd been embarrassed at having him look at her body. Teruo, being a doctor, shared the common belief that after her husband a woman usually feels closest to her family physician. But that didn't mean that he would ever seriously consider using his position to seduce her. He was content with his erotic fantasies.

After dinner, Teruo left on a house call. Naoko went next door for the longest time. Even when Teruo came home, she still hadn't returned. Teruo didn't try to hide his displeasure. He would never have dreamt, of course, that the nineteen-year-old maid Nanase knew all about his jealousy.

Why does this jealousy of mine keep getting worse and worse, Teruo wondered. More than ten years had passed since his wife's dominant personality had started grating on his nerves. He had confidence in his own sexual prowess, and even had the strange conviction that a dark-skinned, muscleman-type like Ichikawa was probably not very good in bed.

He works so hard, that's why I feel inferior, Teruo thought. He had heard from both his wife and Mrs Ichikawa how Shogo would stay up several nights in a row slaving away on some job that wasn't particularly profitable.

And he's a sort of craftsman who has little interest in social status or money – that, too, must be a source of my sense of inferiority.

When Naoko came home, Teruo tried hard to act unconcerned. In the back of her mind, Naoko knew what he was feeling, but she was also floating on air thanks to her long conversation with Shogo. She didn't have a thought for Mrs Ichikawa, who must have been there the whole time. Obviously she had ignored her.

That night Nanase was disturbed by the couple's unusually passionate lovemaking. The living room separated Nanase's small room from their bedroom so she couldn't hear anything. But the consciousnesses of the couple absorbed in the act took over the entire three-bedroom apartment, and Nanase's own curiosity made it impossible for her to let down the latch completely.

While Teruo made love, Naoko fantasized about Shogo. She could only desire her husband when Shogo's image still burned vividly in her mind. Teruo, aware of this, was trying his best to conjure up Mrs Ichikawa's image.

Nanase didn't have the composure, however, to see the humour in the strange harmony of these rising curves. For the sexually inexperienced Nanase, the Takagis' self-deception was indecent. And of course, they were deceiving each other as well. Nanase had been subjected to such sexual games in various households, and something more than the mere fastidiousness of a teenager had hardened her superego. For quite a while she had felt that she would never get married.

The next day, Nanase took her belongings to the Ichikawas. The layout of their apartment was identical to that of the Takagis', and Nanase was given the same small room.

However, the Ichikawa living room was in quite a different state from the Takagis': it had become more of a workroom than a living room. Samples of building materials, catalogues, blueprints and estimates were piled up on the furniture and the floor. One corner was taken up with a big steel desk used for drafting and a side table for materials.

Shogo had been hired to do the design of a supermarket to be built in the old part of the city. And he had been given only one week to complete the project. His two assistants would take care of the smaller jobs in his tiny office while he spent the week at home, devoting himself day and night to the supermarket contract.

After helping out the Ichikawas for several days, Nanase realized why Mrs Ichikawa needed a maid. Shogo was far from being a tyrant, but if anything got in the way of his work, he'd invariably blow up. His eating and sleeping habits were irregular. When engrossed in work, he often wouldn't touch his food. But when he did feel like eating, no matter what time of the day or night, he'd get angry if nothing was ready. So either Takako or Nanase would have to stay up at night. In the daytime, visitors would come calling from the morning on, which meant that both Takako and Nanase had to be awake to receive them. Even if they tried sleeping in shifts, the constant ringing of the telephone in the small three-bedroom apartment made it impossible to do so much as doze.

The mild-mannered Takako was quite incapable of responding quickly to her husband's demands, which annoyed Shogo no end.

"Featherbrain," he'd shout at his wife abusively.

Why can't you be more like Mrs Takagi?

He wasn't crass enough to say this out loud, but Takako knew what he was thinking. She had suffered listening to the dizzying, intellectual, quick-fire conversations he would have with Naoko. But she was also well aware that she could never imitate Naoko's style. Takako, the only daughter in an old-fashioned, loving household, had always obeyed her husband; however, she had begun to find his increasing short-temperedness more than she could handle, and now she was in desperate need of gentle affection. So for her, Dr Takagi was the ideal man. As Takako saw it, her husband's temperament might strike some as manly, but in fact it was more a display of feminine hysteria. In a sense she was correct. For her, real manliness meant love and concern for a woman. She could feel it in someone like Dr Takagi – good-natured and stable and kind. And here too she was correct in a sense.

Nanase, whose telepathy had turned her into a people watcher of no mean ability, was well aware that every personality had its good and bad elements. But for two couples to have such clearly opposing viewpoints of each other's strengths and weaknesses was unusual.

Nanase had long believed that in spite of all the misunderstandings and illusions one might have concerning another person, there was bound to be a grain of truth. That didn't mean that if these two couples switched partners they would be able to make a better go of it. They might even end up in a worse state.

It's worth making the experiment, thought Nanase. I'll light their fires and watch what happens.

Left to themselves, they would do nothing. The four were too sensible to act rashly. But if they were remaining loyal to their respective spouses merely out of a surface morality, then this could easily be destroyed – with a bit of help from Nanase's power.

Even if by some chance her scheme ended in disaster for the two couples, Nanase was not about to feel guilty. Obviously, her superego differed from an ordinary person's. Her morality could not accept such a wide gap between a normal person's "desires" and "actions".

For Nanase, there was nothing immoral about making it easier for people's fantasies to become reality. She was motivated more by a strict puritanism in regard to human relations and a spirit of enquiry into the workings of the mind. Since Nanase lacked any conception of "God", she had no qualms about substituting her own actions for the workings of the Almighty. No matter how outrageously she behaved, she would feel neither trepidation nor remorse.

At the Ichikawas' she was kept busy with the housework, but occasionally she did have some free time while Shogo was engrossed in his work. In such instances, Takako and Nanase relaxed and made idle chit-chat. Takako would ply Nanase for information about the Takagis. Of course, she'd ask only roundabout questions so Nanase wouldn't think anything odd, but Nanase could tell from reading Takako's mind that Takako was really curious about Dr Takagi's personal life.

"During his break from one to two, the doctor always goes to the coffee shop on the ground floor of the building. The mistress is almost never home then."

Nanase let this out, knowing that Takako was in the habit of going shopping during that time.

Takako's heart skipped a beat. She resolved to finish her shopping early the next day, and then go to the coffee shop. Takako was convinced that Teruo would call out to her, and even if they were seen together, no one would think it odd that she was talking to her family doctor.

I'll ask him about my insomnia.

Takako was trying to justify herself.

It's not serious enough to go to the trouble of having a check-up. I'm sure that he'd be happy to help me. He wouldn't think badly of me.

Nanase had decided that Takako's heart was the first one she had to set aflame. Naoko's flame would be the easiest to get going, so Nanase could take her time with her.

That day, around six in the evening, after making sure Naoko wasn't home, Nanase went to the Takagis' to pick up some cosmetics she had deliberately left behind. Teruo, just back from the clinic, was all alone. He wasted no time asking Nanase for a cup of tea.

The same as ever, thought Nanase.

He was trying to detain her so he could pump her about the Ichikawas.

While Nanase was serving the tea, he looked up from his report and asked her how it was going next door, acting as if the question had just popped into his head.

"Oh, I'm very busy." Nanase sat down on the sofa, facing Teruo, pretending she was tired.

"Hmm. Sounds rough." As if to encourage Nanase to say more, Teruo put his report aside, took up his teacup and peered into its bottom.

"Mrs Ichikawa has insomnia."

"That could be a problem. Tell her to come to the clinic when she has some free time."

"All right."

"Do they get a lot of callers?"

"Yes, all day long. Oh, sometimes Mrs Takagi drops by to see how I'm doing." Nanase hoped to stir up Teruo's jealousy.

She's incorrigible.

Teruo frowned, but he didn't say anything.

Obviously she isn't going over to talk to Mrs Ichikawa. It's him she wants to see. In that case, why don't I ask Mrs Ichikawa out for dinner? I've had my fill of Naoko's awful cooking. I'll tell her to her face that I ate at a restaurant. But I wonder if Mrs Ichikawa has any free time.

"I feel so sorry for Mrs Ichikawa. She has no time for herself," Nanase jumped in.

"Is that so?" Teruo looked disappointed.

Then I'll have to make my move when she comes for a check-up. But who knows when that will be.

Nanase laughed to herself. When Teruo meets Takako tomorrow at the coffee shop, he'll be sure to make the most of the opportunity.

To arouse Teruo's sympathy, Nanase mentioned that Shogo sometimes yelled at Takako hysterically. Nanase realized that she might be speaking out of line, but she also knew that Teruo wasn't likely to repeat any of this to Naoko.

When Takako came home the next day, shortly after two, her pale cheeks were flushed. She had agreed to have lunch with Teruo the following day at a fancy restaurant in a nearby hotel. Takako was excitedly going over her conversation with Teruo, without seeming to feel the least hint of guilt. Feelings of superiority to Naoko were even budding inside her. It occurred to Nanase that this might be a big step for the quiet Takako. Inside the ego of someone used to being called an "idiot" and a "featherbrain" by her husband, narcissism and self-respect had suddenly reasserted themselves. She had never considered herself in the same class as Naoko, who was intellectual, tall and so much more beautiful, but now she began to see Naoko as inferior to her. And on recalling the haughty way Naoko ignored her – which had not particularly bothered her up until now – she was even brimming over with a lust for revenge. Although this had been appeased to some degree by Teruo's indirect complaints of his wife, and indirect praises of her, she felt the need for something more substantial.

But these emotions had yet to appear on the surface of Takako's consciousness. She was still busy justifying her own actions.

It's nothing. We're just having lunch so he can give me the medication. The only time I can see him is during his lunch break. "I heard from the maid that you have insomnia." *I wonder if Nana volunteered the information or if he specifically asked her about me.* "We can't have that. Let me give you some medication." "That's so kind of you, but since I have to be able to get up at any time, I can't take anything that will put me into a deep sleep." *That was a stupid reply. And he was being so considerate.* "Yes, I also heard from the maid how busy you are. Don't worry. I won't give you sleeping pills – just something to calm your nerves." "Thank you so much. It's nice of you to be concerned." *I wonder if he thought I was being sarcastic.* "You're so reserved. Just the opposite of my wife." *He smiled. Smiled gently. Like an idiot, I could only muster up a half-smile.* "Can you usually get away at this time?" "Uh, yes, well, after shopping, for a bit." *That wasn't much of an answer. Oh, I feel so embarrassed.* "I take my break now. I really should examine you, but..." "No, that's all right. I just need some medication." *Oh, what a curt reply. I'm sure he thought I was being unfriendly.* "Then why don't I give you the medication around this time tomorrow? Oh, I have an idea. I always have my lunch now, so why don't we eat together? Good food is important for sound sleep." *He seemed so calm, and I was so keyed up.*

Takako, thinking about the conversation and what to wear the next day, was in a constant fog. Nanase observed this with deep interest. Naturally, Shogo's rantings became even louder. But Shogo didn't notice that Takako had a different, dreamy look in her eyes, or find it suspicious that her mind seemed to be occupied with something else. He was busy with the interior design, his weak point, and so he was in a particularly intolerant mood. Several weeks had passed since they had had marital relations.

When Takako returned home the next day, her face was even more flushed and she was in even more of a state than the day before. She no longer had a thought for the trivial household matters that usually filled her head. Her mind was taken up with her conversation with Dr Takagi. Teruo Takagi's fat face had got even bigger, now occupying her entire plane of consciousness.

Her heart aflame, Takako recalled how on leaving the hotel restaurant they had both lost their composure when the cashier asked them for their room number, assuming that they were a married couple staying at the hotel.

If Dr Takagi and I were married... If we were and he had taken me to our hotel room...

When Takako thought this far, she felt her body temperature rise. Her fantasy had so excited her that she stood up in confusion, bumped her knees against the coffee table and knocked over a teacup. Then, abruptly awoken from her reverie, she looked about her nervously.

It's finally turned into the real thing, thought Nanase, who was finding Takako both a bit amusing and a bit pathetic. Takako, acting as if she had never been in love before, seemed bewildered by her own mental state.

He invited me out for lunch again tomorrow. I hope it continues... If it continues, what will happen, I wonder.

When Takako imagined having sexual intercourse with Teruo, her eyes took on a gleam.

Every time the word "unfaithful" appeared in her mind, Takako would quickly drive it away. She had always believed that infidelity depended on the feelings of the person in question, regardless of whether sex was involved. As the old-fashioned Takako saw it, just having lunch with another man without telling your husband could be considered being unfaithful. Be that as it may, she felt her relationship with the kind Dr Takagi was of quite a different nature. Even when she imagined having sex with Dr Takagi, she was able to think of it as otherworldly, an aesthetic experience unrelated to such filthy concepts as infidelity and adultery. What never occurred to Takako was that this way of thinking in itself might very well be the first sign of infidelity.

Shogo wrapped up his work at home in a week, and Nanase returned to the Takagis.

"You poor dear. You must be so tired," said Naoko. She had never considered the nineteen-year-old girl worthy of her attention, but now she was treating her with a sickening familiarity. "You can take it easy." Her intentions were only too obvious. Nanase came out with what Naoko wanted to know without waiting to be asked the indirect questions.

"Mr Ichikawa will be working at the construction site starting tomorrow."

"Oh, he won't be in his office?" Naoko, who had been thinking of visiting him there, looked a little disappointed. "But aren't they just laying the foundations for the supermarket?"

"No, I meant the big foreign-goods store that's going up in the neighbourhood. I hear that the work is nearly finished." Nanase had passed by the site once, where work was already progressing on the interior design.

"I had no idea Mr Ichikawa had done the design there too."

Naoko mentally licked her lips. She would just happen to pass by and invite Shogo out. Nanase experienced no small thrill in discovering that Naoko was fantasizing about taking Shogo to the same restaurant in the same hotel where her husband would be enjoying lunch with Mrs Ichikawa. It was entirely conceivable that the two couples would run into each other; if that happened, then so be it, thought Nanase. The incident might spur them into acting more decisively, or, conversely, might dissolve into a big argument that would put a quick end to everything. In either case, Nanase would not be personally affected, and however the situation might develop, it was bound to be interesting.

Teruo no longer tried to question Nanase about Mrs Ichikawa, who had already made it quite clear that she liked him. By thinking about her, he was preening himself inwardly, luxuriating in a happy self-satisfaction. Again and again he would imagine undressing Mrs Ichikawa and having intercourse with her. It was an obscenely graphic fantasy. Even Nanase, who was used to such male fantasies, couldn't help grimacing at the string of lewd images.

Sometimes Teruo would break out grinning, but Naoko never noticed. Since seeing Mrs Ichikawa, he had been paying more attention to his clothes, but the haughty Naoko was oblivious to this too.

The next day – that is, just before noon on the day Teruo had arranged to have lunch with Takako – Naoko rushed off to Shogo's construction site. Provided that Shogo didn't suggest going to some other restaurant he liked, the two couples were bound to meet each other in the hotel.

At precisely two in the afternoon, when Nanase was alone in the living room, a telephone call came from Naoko.

"Hello, Nana. It's me. Is my husband there?" She was trying hard to maintain her usual calm tone, but she was undoubtedly upset. Although Nanase couldn't read her mind over the telephone, it was obvious that Naoko and Shogo had run into Teruo and Takako at the restaurant. Nanase almost burst out laughing as she imagined the spectacle of the four reduced to a state of shock.

"No, he isn't back yet," she answered, stifling her laughter. "He should be at the clinic now."

"I know that much," Naoko snapped and slammed down the receiver.

Judging by her mood, I doubt things went very well with Shogo either, thought Nanase. Probably the shock of seeing the husband she had scorned together with the woman she had scorned was so great that it had driven Shogo out of her thoughts. That such an encounter could have brought Naoko and Shogo closer together was inconceivable.

Several minutes later there was another phone call, this time from Teruo.

"Hello. Oh, it's me." His voice was shaking. "Is Naoko there?"

"No, she isn't back yet."

"Oh... Uh... I see. Well... thanks."

He also hung up immediately. All fearful and trembling, he must have cut a ridiculous figure in front of Takako. Of course, Takako herself would have been in too much of a state to have given Teruo any thought. But as to who made the biggest scene, surely Teruo won hands down.

Nanase giggled. What an unfortunate spot for them to have met. That it was a hotel made them look all the more guilty.

Teruo seemed to have gone to the clinic. Naoko came home first. She was burning with jealousy. Until now, she had never once been jealous over her husband, but the fact that his partner was Mrs Ichikawa made her explode. If her husband had been carrying on with some unknown woman, she probably wouldn't have felt anything.

I'm sure she's been making fun of me all this time.

For some reason, Naoko assumed that her husband and Mrs Ichikawa had been seeing each other for a while already. And of course, she was convinced that they were having sex.

They've been carrying on in the hotel during his lunch breaks!

Imagining this scene drove Naoko into a frenzy. Whatever Nanase said, she was no longer composed enough to reply. For Nanase's benefit, she made a pretence of throwing herself into housework, but her eyes sometimes glazed over and her hands shook constantly. Shogo Ichikawa never appeared in her thoughts. From the moment he saw his wife, Shogo's mood had turned sullen, turning 180 degrees. He was no longer of any concern to Naoko. She could only recall over and over Teruo's panic-stricken face and Takako's look of terror when she ran into them as they were leaving the restaurant.

They must have had good reason to be so upset. I wonder if they had already had sex, or if they were going to their hotel room. Now that they've been found out, they have nothing to lose.

Naoko's face twitched convulsively.

She no longer knew what she was doing. She gave up on housework, sat down on the living-room sofa, and started chain-smoking.

I've got to stay calm until he gets back. What should I say to him? I wonder what he'll say. I'm also at a disadvantage. They could be suspecting us too.

Naoko began to think that keeping quiet might be the best course of action. Since she didn't want him to make a fool out of her, she should just stare at him and grin.

The first one to act jealous loses. He'll probably just grin at me too. If he's going to suspect me anyway, then I'm better off making him suspicious, so we can be on equal terms. I won't be made a fool of. Better not to say anything – grin. Better not to do anything.

It was already evening when Naoko, after all this meandering, finally decided on the stance she'd take towards her husband.

Teruo came home.

He was clearly frightened. Of course, if his wife pounced on him in anger, he was mentally prepared to turn the tables on her. But if it came to a full-fledged argument, he had no confidence that he could out-talk her. Teruo's show of respectability had become second nature, so there was nothing he found more demoralizing than arguing with a woman.

Besides which, he was overcome by an uncontrollable jealousy. Strangely enough, this jealousy, uniting with his libido, had turned into a burning sexual desire for Naoko.

Teruo was disillusioned with Takako. After the incident she had started sobbing. Even as a passing fancy, how could I have been interested in such a childish, helpless woman, thought Teruo, disregarding his own hysterics at the time.

Nanase imagined that Takako was even more disillusioned. Teruo could act like a gentleman when it suited his own interest, but when the chips were down he'd only think about himself. He probably made no attempt to comfort the poor woman.

Teruo and Naoko looked at each other, grinning in unison, and then turned away.

So I was right.

So she is sleeping with him.

At least we can avoid making a scene in front of the maid, they thought with relief, when a new wave of intense jealousy suddenly assailed them both. Stealing glances at each other, they drowned themselves in their bleak delusions.

I wonder what she's like. Better than me?

I can't believe he's more potent than I am.

She's smaller than me.

Maybe he's really something.

These virginal types are the most passionate.

I wonder how much she moans with him.

Just how infatuated is he?

What do they look like in bed?

I wonder if they slept together today.

She might have some marks somewhere.

They were unable, however, to confirm in words what they were thinking. The first one to ask would become the object of ridicule. During dinner and for the rest of the evening, they simply watched television without saying a word to each other. It was risky to say anything – especially in front of Nanase – because the other person might react in anger. Even an innocuous comment involved great risk, for neither one knew if the other was lying in wait for some opportunity to lash out. Their silence went on interminably. When alone in their bedroom, they were still unable to confirm anything in words. There was only one way left. They would seek confirmation through their bodies.

Again that evening, Nanase was disturbed by the couple's erotic consciousness flowing from their bedroom. Even if she couldn't actually see it, she could tell that their lovemaking was more intense than ever. The jealousy they both felt towards each other's lover had given new impetus to the sexual act. To some degree, they were trying to outdo their rival lover, but, more than that, they were enacting a kind of revenge by torturing each other physically.

So that's how she cried out.

So that's how he grabbed at her hair.

By confirming the accuracy of their fantasies, their passion reached new heights.

He couldn't have done this.

His tongue?!

So that's how it was.

He's thinking of her now...

His sweat.
Her legs, like this. Her.
Him. She's thinking of him.
I'll put her out of his mind.
I'll make mincemeat of you.
"More."
I won't let go of you until you're a wreck.
Him.
"Ohh…"
I'm not going to play second fiddle to her.

Momentary ecstasy and loss of self. Flashing light. Heavy breathing. Sweatsweatsweat. A hollow feeling. Smiling at each other shyly.

And yet love had returned to the couple. You could even call it true marital love. They both sensed this. She thought of him as her husband and he thought of her as his wife. Their feelings of indifference, ridicule and fear had been completely washed away.

I've lost, thought Nanase.

It was as if Nanase had helped consolidate the bonds between the couple just as they were about to dissolve. Nanase was convinced that with some small differences in detail the same scene was taking place with the Ichikawas next door. I have a lot to learn about the complexities of the human mind, Nanase thought wryly, as she pulled the quilt up to her chin.

That her experiment had produced such an un-expected result could certainly be considered a defeat for Nanase. But what have I lost to, Nanase wondered.

Obviously not to boundless love. I haven't lost to morality, ethics or sound judgement either.

That's it, she realized. I've lost to the unconscious cunning of the middle-aged. The desperation of the middle-aged couple who, in order to maintain almost non-existent marital ties, would even use each other's infidelities as a way to heighten the sexual act; the flounderings of a middle-aged couple shamelessly trying to hold on to the ecstasy of unbridled sex; the indolence of a middle-aged couple trying to convince themselves that their partner is the only one for them – really just a convenient excuse for their unconscious acceptance of the morality of a monogamous society; in short, the psychology of a middle-aged couple raised and nurtured on prosperity, peace and leisure seeking an outlet for their strong sexual drives – this is what had defeated Nanase.

The next morning, Nanase, about to go shopping, ran into Takako in the hallway. Her sleeves rolled up, she was hard at work washing down her apartment door. There was a big bruise under her eye where her husband must have hit her. And yet Takako looked happier than ever before.

7

*The Sunday
Painter*

"Mr Takemura? You must mean the artist Tenshu Takemura. He lives over there – in the house behind the gas station."

Nanase was confused. The lady who ran the appliance store at the edge of the shopping district referred to Takemura as an artist, but Nanase's former employer had said that he headed an accounting department. Oh well, probably a Sunday painter, Nanase thought. Still "Tenshu" had the ring of a professional name. And if he really were an ordinary businessman, why should he be known in the neighbourhood as an artist?

The Takemura residence was a hotchpotch – a decaying main house, a garishly painted cottage and, visible from the gate, a Western-style atelier tucked away in the garden, back to back with the gas station. The name on the gate read "Tenshu Takemura" – so it actually was his name.

"You worked for the Takagis? As their maid?" "You did?" "Miss Hita, is it?" "You've come for the maid's job?" "Yes, I see." "Oh really?"

While Nanase introduced herself, Toshi Takemura kept up a string of unnecessary responses to everything she said. It was almost as if she was trying to stop Nanase from talking. Repeating the word "maid" in rapid succession, she showed Nanase into the living room.

Toshi was a slender woman whose face betrayed tremendous strength of will. Nanase sighed. Once again, she'd probably end up getting badly hurt and in return have to hurt someone even more.

"We had a servant once before, when my father-in-law was still alive. We've wanted a servant – I mean, a maid – for some time now. But I hear all sorts of things. You know, that young servants – uh, young maids – are all spoilt nowadays. They expect to be treated as one of the family. I heard a horror story about a maid who demanded that she go to dressmaking school. So I kept putting it off. But Mrs Takagi told me you weren't like that. And the housework's been piling up."

Toshi sat down directly in front of Nanase. Her tone made her feelings clear: Nanase should consider it an honour to be a live-in maid at the Takemuras'. She was also intentionally saying "servant" and then correcting herself with "maid". Nanase didn't have to read her mind to figure out that Toshi was trying to intimidate her by showing her she was the boss.

I will not treat her like an equal. A maid is a maid. If she doesn't understand the difference in our social standing, we won't be able to maintain family tradition. The Takemuras are an illustrious family. We go back a long way. But even if I tried to explain, a young girl like this wouldn't understand. Humph, uppity young girls.

Annoyed at Nanase's unchanging expression, Toshi grew more and more antagonistic. She had arbitrarily concluded that Nanase was a typical "uppity young girl".

She won't say anything. I wonder if she wants to complain. Maybe she's sulking. Or maybe she's just weak in the head.

"Uh... excuse me," said Nanase, realizing that this misunderstanding of Toshi's would only get worse if she kept quiet. "When I asked for directions at the appliance shop, I was informed that Mr Takemura is an artist."

"Oh."

Toshi suddenly noticed that Nanase spoke unusually well for a nineteen-year-old girl. Caught slightly off guard, she answered with an ambiguous smile. On the one hand, Toshi liked to boast that her husband was well known even as a Sunday painter; on the other, she looked down on him for not painting as well as his father, Nessa, and not establishing himself as a professional artist. She despised him for not living up to her expectations.

"My husband works for a company during the week and paints on Sundays. His father was a famous artist in the Japanese style, but my husband only paints abstracts in oils. His paintings don't sell, so he has to work for a company."

Toshi wrinkled her nose disdainfully at the word "company", then abruptly changed her tack. She wanted to make sure Nanase knew that the Takemuras were as illustrious as ever. "Even so, my husband has a fine reputation," she quickly added. "Last year he did the illustrations for a newspaper serial." Toshi did not mention that it was an obscure provincial paper.

Just from reading Toshi's mind, however, Nanase could not tell what kind of person Tenshu was.

An artist's temperament. Too trusting. No flexibility. Thinks only of his paintings. Knows nothing of the world.

These thoughts flitted through Toshi's mind, but they couldn't be taken at face value.

So "Tenshu" was his real name after all. Probably his father had given it to him. Hoping his son would follow in his footsteps. But for an oil painter specializing in abstracts, "Tenshu" was not very appropriate.

"Your job won't be difficult," Toshi continued. "We're a small family. Katsuki, our son, lives in the cottage. All he does is sleep or play mah-jong. And that's the whole family. Just the three of us. Your job will be easy."

Your salary's too high.

Earlier Toshi said the housework was "piling up"; now she was saying how "easy" the job would be. This time, Nanase sensed, she was telling the truth. Toshi had decided to hire a "servant" as a way of restoring the appearance of the family's former grandeur. She was a vain and intractable woman. Even after twenty years, she couldn't forget how she had been pampered when she came as a young bride into the house of the master painter Nessa Takemura.

Nanase was given a dark, two-mat room that had been used for storage. There was just enough space for her to spread out her bedding. She had lived in a number of homes before, but this was the worst. There was a closet, but no desk or lamp. These were probably the same conditions servants had to put up with in this house twenty years before. As Nanase arranged her belongings, it occurred to her that if she really were an ordinary maid, she would have already left in a huff.

No guests were expected and no washing had to be done, so once Nanase had prepared dinner, according to Toshi's instructions, she had nothing to do.

Tenshu returned from work a little after six in the evening.

Of normal height and build, he seemed like a good-natured man who was always slightly smiling. He was ten years older than Toshi.

As he stood by the entrance to the living room staring awkwardly at Nanase, Toshi spoke sharply to him, "Don't just stand there – sit down!"

I won't give you the chance to complain.

"This is Nana, the maid. She started working for us today."

"What?" Naturally, Tenshu was taken aback. This was the first time he had heard anything about hiring a maid.

Nanase expected that Tenshu would make some kind of objection. She figured he'd say something mild like "Do we really need a maid?" or "We can hardly afford the luxury" or "Why didn't you discuss this with me before?" Even the most submissive of husbands would say that much. But Tenshu didn't utter a word. This wasn't because Toshi was glaring at him to keep him from speaking. On the contrary, he was staring at his wife as if he were looking at something totally incomprehensible.

When Nanase, sitting upright by the table, peered quickly into Tenshu's mind, she had a bit of a shock. She had never seen a consciousness like this before.

Toshi's face, as reflected in Tenshu's consciousness, was suddenly flattened out as if a truck had rolled over it. Then the image was transformed into a dark-green rectangle with four sharp corners. The rectangle had no eyes, nose or mouth. But whenever Toshi said anything, one of the pointy corners of the rectangle would quiver – so Nanase could tell that the rectangle in Tenshu's mind was his wife!

This was the first time Nanase had glimpsed the consciousness of an abstract painter – and one who, judging by his ability for abstraction, could be considered a professional. But she could not believe that all abstract artists had minds like this. For no matter how much time elapsed, the four-sided figure in Tenshu's mind never reverted to Toshi's real face.

That wasn't the half of it. When Tenshu sat down at the dinner table, the objects before him assumed an odd assortment of geometric shapes. His rice bowl became a chrome yellow trapezoid with a thick white border; his boiled fish in its oblong plate turned into a honeycomb in shades of brown.

Tenshu was eating in a state of total abstraction. Toshi's story of how she had hired Nanase did not register in his mind as words, her voice producing only the smallest of changes in the overall colour of his consciousness. Nanase combed through Tenshu's mind, but she could not find the least trace of anger or resentment towards Toshi.

"You're staring into space again."

Just as you always do.

"Are you listening?"

Acting above us all. Posing as an artist. Even though you have no talent.

Toshi glared at her husband, full of hate.

Yet Tenshu kept eating in silence. One might have interpreted his attitude as a kind of schizophrenic apathy, where he remained completely indifferent to changes in the outside world, or a kind of autism. But both Nanase and Toshi were well aware this was not the case. Tenshu was deliberately, methodically, shutting out the world.

"Humph. Pretending not to hear."

Whenever it's to your advantage, or we have some problem to discuss, you act like you're deaf.

"I can't stand it any more," Toshi spat out, giving up trying to talk to him.

169

Of course, someone who could not read minds like Nanase would have no inkling of the images floating around in Tenshu's head. It was only natural for Toshi to interpret Tenshu's silence as hostile. How could she imagine that he was converting people and objects into abstractions to protect himself from the hostility surrounding him!

This is an amazing talent! Nanase thought. Tenshu is probably sensitive, naive and vulnerable – *not* "posing as an artist", as Toshi likes to think. He was using his special ability as a defence mechanism, as a way to maintain his artistic purity. While Nanase felt sorry for him, she also respected him for discovering this talent within himself.

It was easy to imagine how the sensitive Tenshu had been abused by his wife. Worries at work, the burden of having a famous artist for a father, the impossible expectations and lack of understanding of everyone around him, culminating in their selfish disappointments – these wounds must have run deep. Nanase had no idea when he had adopted this defence mechanism, or how long it had taken him to develop such a singular power. Perhaps it had all come about naturally, without his even being aware of it, under the burden of these interminable attacks on his artistic pride.

Was she overestimating the nature of the artist or just falling prey to sentimentality? Nanase wasn't sure. But she couldn't come up with any other explanation.

She herself had often wanted to shut out the hostile thoughts that invaded her mind non-stop, so Tenshu's ability posed very interesting possibilities.

Toshi started to speak again, still getting no response. The longer Tenshu kept quiet, the more Toshi wanted to scream at him. Any reticence she might have felt in front of Nanase paled before her desire to revile her husband.

"Since we've hired a maid, you're going to have to produce more paintings that can sell."

I know what he's thinking: "this was your decision, so leave me out of it." Well, I won't let him say it. If he makes even the smallest objection, I'll give it to him.

Toshi had the habit of imagining how people might react to her rantings even before they said anything, and then driving herself into a frenzy over it. For her, Tenshu's silence was more galling and humiliating than any complaint he might have uttered. Toshi's pent-up fury was now on the verge of exploding. She couldn't put it into words, but she felt as if her vanity was being laid bare and ridiculed.

Nanase, the third party, had vanished from Toshi's reasoning. Her hand holding the chopsticks trembled violently.

"Why don't you say something!" she screamed, letting her venom out. Her eyes were aflame.

The images in Tenshu's mind started blinking – a warning signal that he had better make some reply.

"Right, right."

"What do you mean 'Right, right'?" Toshi said, grimacing.

I won't put up with being ignored by this idiot.

She picked up a boiled potato and shoved it into her mouth. At least her anger hasn't affected her appetite, Nanase observed.

This seemed to calm Toshi down a bit, and once Tenshu sensed this, he resumed his mechanical eating. Of course, he must have been aware that his silence only made her more angry. But if he spoke rashly to her, she'd lash out at him with greater force, and he'd end up more abused. The best thing to do was to keep quiet. Tenshu had learnt from bitter experience that any argument would drag both of them down into a bottomless pit of hate where they would torture each other endlessly.

Nanase wondered whether this could be considered a "crystal consciousness". Was Tenshu someone capable of looking at life through a philosopher's eyes? For Nanase, Tenshu came closer to this state than anyone she had met before. This was because Nanase had so often glimpsed the ugliness in the hearts of people revered as saints by the world at large.

As Nanase's feelings of goodwill and respect for Tenshu grew, she began to wonder how she herself appeared in his mind. Careful study of his thoughts during dinner revealed that she was nothing more than a white speck on the horizon of his consciousness. Nanase was both disappointed and relieved. White seemed to indicate feelings of amiability, at least if the colours of the other figures in his mind were any indication.

Dinner over, Nanase was carrying dishes into the kitchen when the son, Katsuki, entered the living room. Katsuki was slightly shorter than his father, skinny, and had a smile brimming with contempt and meanness. One glimpse into his mind made it clear to Nanase that Katsuki had inherited his mother's aggressive, self-centred wilfulness. But for Nanase, Katsuki was much more of a threat. From the moment he spotted her, he stared lewdly at her body. His mind oozed with sexual secretions. Nanase particularly disliked this type of consciousness.

"Who's this?" Katsuki gestured with his chin at Nanase, leering at her across the table. "Did you hire a maid?"

"Uh-huh," Toshi answered indifferently. She could not shake off her anger at Tenshu.

"She's beautiful. What a waste, being a maid."

Katsuki was trying to catch Nanase's eye. He kept staring at her suggestively. It occurred to Nanase that some women probably found this attractive. Hoping to avoid his eyes, she smiled at him, looking down as she cleared the table. But even managing this small smile required tremendous effort.

Damn, with her around, I can't ask for money.

Katsuki wanted to tap his parents for money to go mountain-climbing.

If they've got enough to hire a maid, why don't they give some to me? Mum's so pretentious.

But Katsuki didn't say anything. He figured he'd be better off scheming with his mother to get his father to paint something marketable.

"Can I fix you a light meal? You must have already eaten with your friends," said Toshi. She also wanted Katsuki on her side.

"OK."

"Nana, will you get out the pickles?"

While Nanase was preparing Katsuki's snack, he started staring at her again.

Why is such a pretty girl working as a maid?

Katsuki's suspicions made Nanase stiffen.

Recently she had begun to sense a certain danger in her own blossoming figure. There was no denying that her looks were the kind men noticed. She was careful to wear plain clothes, use no make-up and keep her hair in a childish style, but she wasn't able to hide her looks any longer.

Why would an attractive girl with a high-school diploma be working as a maid? Anyone aware of the labour shortage might begin to wonder. Even if such a doubt did not directly result in the discovery of Nanase's ESP powers, there was ample danger. For Nanase had become a household maid precisely because it was a job where she could move easily from place to place without arousing suspicion, all the while avoiding society's prying eyes. I have to be careful, she told herself. I'd better watch Katsuki's mind like a hawk.

"Isn't Dad gonna do any more illustrations for the newspaper?" Katsuki asked his mother. He would always talk about his father as if he were out of the room – a reaction to the way Tenshu always ignored them. Despising this in his father, Katsuki had secretly begun to call him "Helen Keller".

"Not unless they specifically ask him to…" said Toshi, sighing heavily. She was delighted to find Katsuki on the same wavelength as her.

"You must have made a lot of money on that job," Katsuki goaded his father, staring at him.

"Hmm." Tenshu looked at his son with eyes devoid of feeling.

In Tenshu's consciousness, Nanase watched as two concentric circles, the outer one dark green and the inner one orange, suddenly expanded. Apparently the circles represented Katsuki.

He's playing Helen Keller again.

Katsuki screwed up his nose in disgust. His nose was perfect for this – big, flaring nostrils and a tip pointing upwards.

"OK, OK." Katsuki gave up.

What's the point of talking to the moron? He'll just say he doesn't want to do anything commercial. Posing like an artist. What an idiot. Who does he think he is anyway? He's just a fraud. First make some money. Then you can act so high and mighty.

"The ward office has asked him to do a painting," said Toshi with an exaggerated sigh. "They want him to do a large oil to hang over the staircase landing."

If only he'd do it, we'd make a bundle.

In one corner of his consciousness, Tenshu was aware that he was the topic of their conversation, but for him their words were simply hundreds of tiny right-angled triangles appearing and disappearing inside his head.

"Couldn't he sell them one of the big paintings in his studio?" Katsuki asked his mother, excited over his own idea.

"Impossible," Toshi answered, giving Tenshu a nasty stare. "Those crazy paintings are no good. The ward office wants something more realistic."

"Then why don't you paint something more realistic? A real painting that anyone could understand instead of something crazy. Come on, Dad," Katsuki urged. His light-hearted tone made it sound as if he himself would be doing the painting. "You can do it. All you have to do is put your mind to it. It'll be a cinch. Come on, come on."

Katsuki patted his father twice on the shoulder. It was an exaggerated, condescending gesture, and the insolence made even Nanase momentarily furious. But since Tenshu had not allowed Katsuki's words to enter his mind, he didn't register the slightest sign of anger. Tenshu looked up absently and stared at his son as if gazing at an object of little interest.

"Right, right," Tenshu muttered.

What is this "right, right" business?

Katsuki cursed his father inwardly.

You're thinking that art isn't like that. That someone like me can't possibly understand art. That a true artist can't so easily paint to order. Arrogant bastard! I'll put you in your place. You pompous ass.

"You really mean it!" Katsuki exclaimed with feigned cheerfulness, anger boiling inside him. "You can start painting right away. Tomorrow. Better yet, you can start tonight. Wow, I'm so excited. Since it's a commercial painting, you can paint by electric light. I can't wait for you to start." The more Katsuki talked, the more worked up he got – until he could no longer hide his sarcasm. "Wow, this is really great. If you make some money, I can go to the mountains with my friends. You're a wonderful dad."

Those eyes! He has eyeballs like a fish. Why don't you say something? Look how your son is making fun of you. Why don't you try getting angry for a change? I think I'll punch you in the nose. Maybe that'll get a rise out of you.

Nanase suddenly sensed danger. Katsuki was in a rage. His hatred and disdain of his father, now at irrational levels, had tainted his world bright red. Deep down Katsuki knew that he was the one who was selfish and in the wrong. But for this very reason, all morality and restraint had fled elsewhere, leaving his perverse mind out of control. A primitive anger burned inside him. He might actually resort to violence, Nanase thought nervously.

Tenshu as well seemed to have sensed that something was wrong. He began to make an effort to understand what Katsuki was saying. At the very moment when Tenshu's consciousness tuned into the reality around him, Nanase stepped in. "Would you like some more tea?" she asked him.

Immediately, instinctively, Tenshu caught on that Nanase was telling him to get out of the room – and quickly. He seized the opportunity to stand up.

"Uh, no thanks," he said. Then, with remarkable speed, Tenshu dashed out of the poison-filled room, not giving Toshi and Katsuki the chance to pursue their attack.

He's run away, dammit.

Katsuki almost slammed his rice bowl down on the table. He cursed his father furiously in his mind.

The bastard's run away. I'm not good enough to talk to.

"No matter how we plead, it's hopeless," Toshi spit out, her lips quivering.

He's waiting for us to come begging on our hands and knees. I'll never do that. Pompous idiot. He can go to the Devil.

"I'd like to step on his face," Katsuki threw in.

Mother and son were closely bound by their common hatred of Tenshu. Katsuki was graphically imagining beating his father to death while he consumed two bowls of *ochazuke*. He enacted the drama over and over in his mind, changing the details each time.

Nanase was staring at him in disbelief when Katsuki
suddenly lifted his head and their eyes met. He took
the opportunity to look her over suggestively. Nanase
quickly glanced down. Thoughts of his father abruptly
vanished form Katsuki's consciousness and he started
replaying the various scenarios he had come up with
for seducing girls.

*It'll be easy. She's so innocent. From the country.
Obviously inexperienced. No urban sophistication. If I
come on strong. She's just a maid, so I don't have to worry
about the consequences. A movie. The park. Kissing. A
motel.*

Then, in his mind, he began to remove Nanase's
clothing, one article at a time. When she was stripped
of all but her panties, Nanase, still looking downwards,
smirked and went off to the kitchen.

*She smirked at me! Maybe she guessed what I was
thinking. In which case, she might be a real swinger. Nah,
she's not such hot stuff.*

Katsuki had been caught off guard for a moment,
but he would never admit defeat. It was a trait he had
inherited from his mother.

This was the first time Nanase had challenged the
thoughts of someone she found offensive. But she
immediately regretted having taken the chance. That
she would hate Katsuki enough to take such a risk
might be because she had finally met someone she
could actually like. I have to be careful, she cautioned
herself again. I have to watch myself most of all.

Toshi picked up where she'd left off. "Even with the newspaper serial last year," she whined to Katsuki, "it was like pulling teeth. 'I can't do pen drawings, I can't draw people,' he grumbled the whole time. All he did were landscape sketches in pencil. The newspaper editors were appalled. With that kind of attitude, you can be sure he'll never work for a newspaper again. Maybe it's his way of hiding how bad his paintings really are."

How much ability *does* Tenshu have, Nanase wondered while she washed the dishes. She had a feeling that his paintings couldn't be bad, but she wanted to make sure that she wasn't overestimating him.

The very next day she had the chance to find out. Toshi asked her to clean Tenshu's atelier, to wash the windows in the main house and to straighten up Katsuki's cottage. She seemed to have been saving up jobs for Nanase to do.

As soon as she finished breakfast, Nanase went to the atelier. Except for a bit of dust collecting in the corners, the modest-sized room was extremely clean. Judging by the state of the paints, canvases and other equipment, Nanase could tell that Tenshu himself had done the cleaning up until now.

In the centre of the room an abstract painting – evidently a work in progress – sat resting on an easel. As Nanase had imagined, the design consisted of geometric figures. Although the composition itself was extremely erratic, the exciting coloration made the work dynamic. Curiously enough, Toshi and Katsuki were also present among the geometric figures: on the canvas, a dark-green quasi-rectangle and orange and dark-green concentric circles inside a morass of the sepia of everyday life.

Nanase gazed untiringly at the painting, then suddenly wondered whether she found it interesting only because she was aware of the make-up of Tenshu's consciousness. Toshi and Katsuki, of course, could not possibly understand his work. Toshi hated the kind of painting that did not depict real objects, and one glance at Katsuki's cottage told Nanase that his sense of colour was a cut below average.

Nanase felt she had a good eye for art. As she looked through the ten-odd paintings propped up against the wall in the corner, she gained confidence in her notion that if she had seen these paintings without knowing Tenshu himself, she would not have found them great works of art. They were a kind of autobiographical novel in the form of painting – Tenshu's own consciousness preserved on canvas. Even the most perceptive of critics would hardly be likely to comprehend that. Still, this did not mean that the works were failures. The world was inundated with fakes that made free use of superficial, showy techniques. Tenshu completely ignored fashionable styles, and his talent was real.

The stronger Nanase's affection for Tenshu became, the stranger it seemed that he could have fathered such a gross child. Even looking at Katsuki in the best possible light, she could not find in him the merest similarity to his father.

Once again Nanase wondered whether she were overestimating Tenshu. After all, she had only observed him in a state where his perceptions were cut off by his abstraction of his surroundings. How did his consciousness work when he perceived reality? She had no idea how capable he was at his job, but the very fact that he had a managerial position suggested that his ability to judge reality couldn't be all that poor. And considering his mathematical mind, he probably was an extremely capable accountant.

Since it was Saturday, Tenshu came home early. He dropped by the atelier for a moment, then spoke to Nanase, who was working in the garden.

"Did you clean my studio?"

"Yes."

"Thanks," he said, smiling as he walked off to the main house.

Nanase's blush refused to go away. The white dot that represented her in Tenshu's consciousness had expanded into a perfect circle. The situation is getting more and more dangerous, thought Nanase. True, she was pleased that Tenshu showed signs of liking her, but enjoying a man's attentions was a first-time experience for her, and that in itself made her uneasy.

That evening, Nanase avoided eating with the Takemuras. She holed herself up in her room, reading. She couldn't bear to watch Tenshu being bullied by his family, and she was afraid that she might impulsively say or do something imprudent in order to protect him.

Toshi seemed displeased that Nanase wasn't serving dinner, but did not demand that she do it. If Nanase were present, she couldn't abuse Tenshu to her heart's content. The next day was Sunday – the day Tenshu spent painting in his atelier – so she had to badger him into doing the commercial paintings before the night was over. Nanase predicted that the air in the dining room would get even more poisonous than the night before. Still, no matter how his family reviled or pleaded with him, Tenshu wasn't likely to give in. Nanase laughed to herself: Tenshu's ability to transcend his surroundings made a farce of his scheming family.

As expected, Toshi and Katsuki's joint attack lost easily to Tenshu's silence. When Nanase was certain that Tenshu and Katsuki had retreated to their own rooms, she went into the kitchen. She found Toshi furiously washing the dishes, a storm of curses raging in her heart.

The idiot. The idiot. What kind of man is he? Doesn't he want the money? I'll feed him scraps from now on. What enjoyment does he get out of life? He's been spurning me for years. Does he think I'm going to give up so easily? He'll do the painting even if I have to use bodily force. Now, to think of a plan.

How could someone as refined as Tenshu possibly find his obnoxious wife attractive? It figured that they hadn't had sexual relations for several years now. What was startling to Nanase was how happy this revelation made her.

"I want you to hurry up and eat!" Toshi screamed hysterically at Nanase. "How am I going to clean up?"

Nanase found Toshi's violent, indiscriminate anger amusing.

"I'm sorry. I'll do it myself."

Nanase spoke slowly and calmly.

Humph. Smart-alecky bitch. Making fun of me, eh? Wait until you do something wrong – then I'll give it to you.

Toshi glared at Nanase and left the room in a huff.

On Sunday all Tenshu did was a little more work on the painting on the easel. The words "commercial painting" didn't seem to surface even once in his mind. Ready to explode, Toshi and Katsuki waited impatiently for Tenshu to appear at the dinner table.

Again, Nanase holed herself up in her room. This could turn into a nightly routine, she thought. The family seems to have been carrying on this way every night for years. Could you call this dinner? Weren't they just feasting on hatred and anger?

One week passed. On a few rare occasions Nanase was able to glimpse Tenshu's consciousness tuned into reality. While his thoughts struck her as rather precise, they were merely fragments – at best, recollections of something that had happened at the office. They lacked the coherence of thoughts analysing current, real-life situations. Nanase wanted to read Tenshu's mind while he was at work.

On Monday, Nanase took the day off and headed downtown to the shopping district where Tenshu's company was located. In the basement of the building was a large restaurant; Nanase had garnered from a fragment of Tenshu's consciousness that he ate lunch here every day.

When Nanase arrived just before noon, the restaurant was still empty. She took a seat in a corner booth, out of sight of the other tables, and treated herself to a hearty lunch – to make up for the paltry meals she got at the Takemuras'.

The restaurant filled up, but Tenshu was nowhere to be seen. If he did show up, Nanase was sure that she'd be able to pick him out immediately, regardless of the number of customers. She had honed her ability to distinguish, even in a crowd, the thoughts of someone whose consciousness she was already familiar with. If necessary, she could shut out the consciousness of everyone else.

Nanase finished eating. Still no Tenshu. She ordered coffee.

Nanase liked coffee. Whenever she drank coffee, her telepathic powers seemed to grow stronger. She had read that human beings' mental processes were slowed

185

down by barbiturates, but speeded up by caffeine. If caffeine really did increase her power, then she could consider telepathy an advanced function, rather than a residue of primal instinct.

When her coffee arrived, Nanase felt a distinct stirring in her mind. This was a consciousness that she was thoroughly familiar with. She didn't have to turn around to know it was Tenshu, but she wanted to see if he was alone. She peeked at the entrance from behind the screen. Tenshu and two office girls were sitting in a booth right by the entrance. Apparently all the other tables in the restaurant were taken.

Oh no, thought Nanase. She'd have to stay hidden at the table until they left.

The office girls, dressed in smocks, were both in their early twenties. Nanase could only see their hair and shoulders. One had short hair; the other was on the plump side and wore her hair up. From Tenshu's consciousness, she learnt that the girl with her hair up was Takako and that she worked in Tenshu's accounting department. The short-haired girl's name did not enter his thoughts.

After observing Tenshu's consciousness for a while, Nanase realized that he was completely ignoring the girl with the short hair. She had been converted into an orange isosceles triangle with a tapered tip. When her tip occasionally quivered, it meant that she was saying something. But Tenshu's mind was making not the least attempt to comprehend her words. Nanase wondered if he hated this girl – after all, orange was the colour of one the concentric circles that represented Katsuki.

Tenshu's interest was directed solely at Takako. Through Tenshu's eyes, Nanase could see her white skin, dark eyebrows and roundish face. In Tenshu's consciousness, this face would frequently change into a large white circle. If the colour and size of the circle were anything to go by, he obviously had warm feelings for her.

This came as a mild shock to Nanase, but she didn't feel particularly jealous of Takako. In a way she was relieved to confirm that the closeness she had felt for Tenshu was completely unromantic in nature. Anyway, that was the least of her worries now. The undeniable reality she had to face was that her own image of Tenshu had been a gross exaggeration – it was nothing more than an idealized portrait of Tenshu as she herself wanted him to be.

Nanase watched as desire for Takako surfaced in his consciousness – stirrings of pure lust, without an iota of love. Even more disturbing were his thoughts on how to acquire the object of his desire. Takako had misappropriated some company funds, and Tenshu intended to use that information to trap her.

Actually, Tenshu's embezzlement had been more of a prank than anything else. All she had stolen was a few thousand yen for the sake of a girlish thrill. But Tenshu was mulling over how this could be used to blackmail her into sleeping with him. He was her immediate superior and the only one who knew of her embezzlement; she was unmarried and virginal. It would be easy.

Tenshu himself didn't think there was anything at all despicable about this. He converted people into geometric figures simply because he held the whole world in contempt and thought of people as tools for his own ends.

Nanase had observed the egotism of an artist two or three times before, but she had never seen anything like this. She was appalled.

"I just want to even the score. You must, too." Strike out; rewrite. *"I'm sure you must feel the same way. It's better if we each have our own secret."*

Big, white circle.

"I have a family." Don't give her the chance to think it over. *"You're still single."* No, I need an extra something. Timing. Just before we settle accounts. That'll unnerve her. Two days before. When she leaves work. Within the day. After the first shock, gradually lull her into a feeling of security. As soon as she lets down her guard, lure her to a hotel.

Black spots.

Black spots represented Tenshu's sexual desire. Katsuki was his father's son after all.

Of course, Takako had no idea what Tenshu was thinking. Unaware that he had sniffed out her embezzlement, she was laughing and enjoying herself. Little did she know that before long she'd be tormented by an uncalled-for guilt and forced to give herself to Tenshu. Nanase, who almost never felt sorry for anyone, couldn't help pitying her.

With the restaurant full, Nanase could not just sit there indefinitely. She drank a second cup of coffee. When Tenshu went to the restroom, she quickly got up to leave.

At the cash register behind Tenshu's booth, Nanase paid her bill. Briefly she read the minds of the two girls. From a distance of one or two yards, she could easily distinguish between their consciousnesses.

What?! The short-haired girl had had an affair with Tenshu!

It's obvious that the boss likes Takako. Should I warn her? Tell her she'd better watch out for him, that he has a bad reputation for fooling around? No. No way. I can't say anything. What if word got out about my affair with him? The cheat. Giving me all that bull. Deceiving me. He'll give her the same line. What a mistake to get involved with an artist. Then getting pregnant on top of it. He ignored me the whole time, the creep. The indifferent beast. He's turned into a cold-blooded animal.

Once he had satisfied his lust with anyone, Tenshu reduced the person to a hateful orange-coloured existence – annoying, unpleasant and tiresome. Anyone who got in the way of his latest conquest was converted into an abstract shape and ignored. Then, within the secure warmth of his ego, he would indulge in his conquest to his heart's content. Here was the root of his artistic egotism – the narcissism of a man convinced that he was a genius with the right to do whatever he pleased.

Nanase's image of Tenshu had now completely reversed itself. He had turned into someone so ugly and repulsive that the thought of him made her feel physically ill. When she left the restaurant, she realized how much she hated him.

The shopping district was bathed in a languid afternoon sunlight. She walked a dozen metres hurriedly and then entered a phone booth. The booth was hot and stuffy. She took a matchbox from the restaurant out of her handbag and dialled the number on it.

"Could you please page a customer for me – a Miss Takako Ochiai," said Nanase.

Takako soon came on the line. "Yes?"

Nanase spoke slowly, "Today or tomorrow, return the money you embezzled." Then she hung up. That should be enough to get through to her.

Nanase worked for the Takemuras for ten more days.

She had two reasons for quitting. One was that Katsuki was constantly pestering her.

"Where'd you go on your day off?"

"Next Sunday, let's go to a movie."

"Why do you wear your hair like that?"

"You have nice skin."

The more stand-offish she was, the more his passion grew inside him.

The other reason had to do with Tenshu. The white circle representing Nanase in his consciousness continued to get bigger and bigger. After his setback with Takako, his goal shifted to Nanase, the girl closest at hand. He was hanging around her all the time, trying to think of some way to seduce her.

Like father, like son, thought Nanase. Both were indolent, with an abnormally bloated lust for conquest – directed solely at women. In that light, Tenshu's paintings were revolting. The erratic dynamism of the composition was no more than an expression of his warped self-absorption. He painted every Sunday just so he could wallow in the smugness of his ego.

Of course, this may very well be the essence of creative instinct, Nanase reconsidered wryly.

When Nanase announced that she would be leaving, Toshi looked at her askance. Her animosity for "modern uppity young girls" burst forth into her consciousness, and she let loose with an interminable stream of virulence.

"It's just as I thought. You always had this sulking, complaining look about you. Well, if you're going to quit anyway, you're better off doing it now. In spite of the easy work here, you couldn't even last a month, could you?

"There's just one thing I want to say. You'll never be able to work anywhere. Not for very long. It's absolutely out of the question. If it's better treatment you want, then you better learn how to behave like a servant. You'd like a nice room and a big salary, I suppose. You go try and find such a job. You're probably thinking that you only want what any maid wants these days. Well, the Takemuras do not hire maids who act like aristocrats. Servants must know their proper place. Of course, you modern stuck-up girls wouldn't understand. That's why you can't find good maids any more. They run around with boys and end up getting pregnant. You better watch out. Oh, but you're a lost cause. You wouldn't even care. Uppity young girl."

8

*Dear Departed
Mother*

Shintaro Shimizu's heart was awash with tears.

Why did you die? How could you have died and left me? How awful of you! What a terrible mother! What am I going to do now? Why did you die?

These thoughts were completely without logic. Nanase found it hard to believe that this was the consciousness of a twenty-seven-year-old man.

Even though a whole day had passed since the death of Tsuneko, his mother, Shintaro's tear-drenched mind could only haltingly repeat the same phrases over and over.

Why did you die? What am I going to do now? How awful of you! How awful of you to die without me!

Shintaro's tears could best be described as tears of childish self-indulgence. He was trying to console himself by crying non-stop, wallowing in the memories of his dead mother. He had always been coddled by her. Now all he had left were his memories. Nanase wondered if this could really be the same man who graduated from a first-rate university and was working for a top company. She found herself doubting her own telepathic power.

Just how long is he going to keep on crying?

It's as if his entire body is made out of tears. If he cries much longer, his eyes might dissolve.

Nanase felt sorry for Sachie, who was thinking this while watching her husband make a scene in front of everybody. In their three years of marriage, Sachie had been tormented by her husband's abnormal closeness to his mother.

It looks as if I'll have to put up with his crying for a while. But what if he never stops?

When Sachie trembled at the thought that her husband might never be free of memories of his mother, Nanase understood only too well how she felt.

From a pathological viewpoint, Nanase had a better understanding of Shintaro's disorder than Sachie, so she knew that Sachie had good cause for worry. However, Nanase also knew that if ever Shintaro was to "wean" himself from his mother, it could only be through something as drastic as her death. Of course, whether or not Shintaro would be able to stand on his own emotionally depended on his own strength of will.

The funeral guests had spilt out from the living room almost to the veranda. When the memorial service began, Nanase sat up straight at the very back, lowering her head as the priest chanted sutras. Nearly all the friends and relations gathered there seemed aware of Shintaro's mother complex. Many of the guests, looking for something to gossip about, were enjoying Shintaro's abnormal grief and Sachie's reaction.

Sachie looks so happy. She must be relieved.

A grown man carrying on so.

His cheeks are shining with tears.

He doesn't seem to give a hoot about appearances.

He's a child. And he's already twenty-seven – he'll never grow up. Poor Sachie. The end of the Shimizu line.

Sachie looks embarrassed. Her husband's sobbing so much. She should at least make a pretence of crying.

Nanase had started working at the Shimizus' two months earlier, ten days after Tsuneko had taken to her bed. Tsuneko didn't want her daughter-in-law to nurse her, and Sachie didn't like the idea either.

Now that Tsuneko was dead, Sachie did feel as if a weight had been lifted from her shoulders. When Nanase peered into her mind, she found her constantly recalling Tsuneko's abusive treatment in order to alleviate her guilt about how she felt.

Her curses. She hated me. The more I nursed her, the more she hated me. She'd shout so loud the neighbours could hear. "Do you want to kill me? You idiot," she screamed. Non-stop. "You can't nurse someone properly if your heart isn't in it," she screamed.

But when you're hated that much and yelled at that much, how can you keep on caring? It's impossible. Impossible.

Sachie's goodness came out in this angry self-justification. Nanase was impressed with the way she had put up with Tsuneko and Shintaro's maltreatment of her. If Sachie had been a modern, independent young woman, she probably would have got a divorce before a year had passed.

Since Nanase had the ability to know what a patient wanted before he or she said anything, she had the makings of a perfect nurse. She was also a maid par excellence. But when she took over from Sachie, Tsuneko was critical even of her, lashing out at her from her sickbed and making unreasonable demands. Her talent for picking out other people's faults was a constant source of amazement to Nanase; she could hardly blame Sachie for cowering at the thought of having to look after Tsuneko. No matter how devotedly Nanase took care of her by literally anticipating her every need, Tsuneko would brood obsessively in her sickbed, invariably concluding that Nanase's intentions were malicious. Nanase could easily imagine how much Tsuneko had tormented Sachie.

As his mother's condition worsened, Shintaro started going off the deep end. He'd taken days off from work, never leaving his mother's bedside. He hadn't gone to work at all for the six days before she died. Neither did he think there was anything strange about using his mother's illness as an excuse. His superiors could upbraid him and his co-workers could make all the jokes they liked – Mummy was sick and that was ample reason for Shintaro to stay home.

"My boss said that if Mummy died, it'd be one thing, but it's no excuse to stay home just because she's sick."

Nanase was eavesdropping as Shintaro spoke excitedly to Tsuneko.

"So what did you say?"

"I told him I'd take the time off without pay. My boss said it would put him in a bind."

"You should stay away once in a while so they'll appreciate your worth." Tsuneko spoke happily. "Make them suffer."

Shintaro always called Tsuneko "Mummy". She loved it. He made it a rule not to think about the content of his work in front of her. If he dwelt on some technical problem which his mother couldn't understand, her mood would turn sour. But until the day Tsuneko died, he talked about everything else to her, just as if she was his girlfriend.

Shintaro would openly confide his anger and sadness, and seek his mother's advice when he had a problem. He wouldn't try to figure anything out for himself; in fact, he'd even make an effort not to think about anything until he could discuss it with Tsuneko. He'd carry his problems home with him and then drop them on his mother's lap.

Why, that's nothing to get so worked up over. They're all jealous of your abilities. You're too smart. People are bound to resent you. It's a kind of fate. Jealousy towards the elite.

Tsuneko comforted Shintaro and instilled him with confidence. She had become a part of his ego – his superego even. But now Tsuneko was dead.

Mummy. You're an awful mother. Why did you die? You died to make me suffer. Don't you know I'm lost without you, Mummy? Do you want to make me suffer? How mean of you!

For Shintaro, Tsuneko's death was a woman's betrayal of a man. And there wasn't one person who could comfort him by saying otherwise.

Once the chanting was over, Shintaro's hysterical sobbing could be heard throughout the room. Anyone else would have been drowned out by this wailing. But when Nanase extended her telepathic antennae, she couldn't find a single guest who was grieving. Most of them were laughing at Shintaro's ridiculous behaviour.

One of his colleagues who was acting as an usher was having trouble holding in his laughter.

This is no ordinary crying. I'm sure they had an incestuous relationship.

Even as he was recalling some of the sick jokes passed around the office, he put on a grave face. "Now for the offerings of incense. First the son of the deceased, Mr Shintaro Shimizu."

Shintaro didn't even have the strength to stand up. He crawled his way to the altar, his shoulders shaking. The consciousnesses of the guests reverberated with laughter at the sorry spectacle. Sachie grew hot with embarrassment.

Shintaro, his eyes puffed and red from crying, made his offering of incense, all the while ranting senselessly in his mind.

You flung me into this den of wolves. All alone. You ran away from me. I'm not gonna do what you want me to any more. 'Cause you've been a bad Mummy. I'll show you. I'll be a bad boy.

I'll be a bad boy.

When Shintaro was little, Tsuneko always warned him to stay away from bad boys. "Even if they ask you to play with them, just ignore them. If they start pestering you, Mummy will chase them away," she'd say.

But isn't the world full of bad people? You're the one, Mummy, who told me not to have anything to do with them. That's why I don't know what to say to them. You're not to chase them away for me any more, are you?

Shintaro had collapsed in tears in front of the altar. Two male relatives had to drag him away.

Everyone around me is bad. Tell me what to do. Everyone's picking on me. Everyone's laughing at me. Chase them away, Mummy. I don't know how to.

Sachie slowly made her offering of incense three times before Tsuneko's photograph. Tsuneko was wearing rimless glasses and looked younger than her years. Her stern expression stared down at Sachie. When Sachie looked up at it, her heart filled with resentment.

Mother, you lied to me!

Tsuneko had come to Sachie's parents, who ran a large men's apparel store downtown, to suggest marriage between her son and Sachie. Shintaro had been shopping at the store and had been smitten with Sachie, who happened to be helping out there. As he always did whenever he wanted anything, he pleaded with Tsuneko to get her to marry him.

Before the formal marriage meeting, Shintaro did not attempt to speak to Sachie even once. If he had and she had responded coldly, his sensitive ego would have been wounded on the spot. Shintaro was both aware of and afraid of this. Tsuneko took care of everything.

I plan to build a house for Shintaro. I'd just get in the way of the newly-weds. I still have my health, so I'll be fine on my own.

Both Sachie and her parents felt well disposed towards the friendly Tsuneko. Sachie's parents, who were relatively modern, were impressed by the eager and straightforward manner in which Tsuneko proposed the marriage, dispensing with most of the traditional matchmaking fuss. Sachie too saw Tsuneko as a modern-minded mother liberated from tired old customs.

She acted like a saint until we got married. She was always so kind, buying me things. A beautiful engagement ring.

She seemed so easy to talk to. Graduate of a women's academy, intellectual. And rich.

Her late husband headed a group of trading companies. Her son's bright. And quiet. Graduated from a good university top of his class. On an elite track at his company.

Her only son, so, of course, the entire inheritance.

The big house itself is worth a small fortune. Just the land.

The family exchanged such comments among themselves ad infinitum. Six months later, Sachie and Shintaro were married.

However, Tsuneko never kept her promise to build them a house.

Mum's sickly. We've got to live with her. The house is so big anyway.

At first, Shintaro seemed a bit guilty as he made excuses to Sachie. Even if we build a new house, we'll end up moving back here when Mother dies, thought Sachie, and she tried to make the best of it. Of course, if she actually said as much to Shintaro, she knew he would accuse her of waiting for Tsuneko's death. So she kept quiet.

The reality was that Shintaro himself was unable to break away from his mother.

Once Sachie entered the family, Tsuneko's manner changed abruptly, and she started haranguing her daughter-in-law.

We don't need a new house. To go through all that trouble just for her sake. She's a member of our family now. I'm not going to live apart from you.

Tsuneko would talk like this to Shintaro.

She would deliberately speak in a loud voice. She wanted me to hear her. She wanted to torture me.

After finishing her offering of incense, Sachie glared at Tsuneko's photograph for a while.

What on earth am I to this family? A nuisance. An object of hate. Not worthy of their attention. Or am I a toy? A discarded toy? A maid?

One after another, the relatives came up to the altar to offer incense. Nanase couldn't find anyone who was genuinely mourning Tsuneko's death. They still bore grudges from past humiliations, and they recalled incidents when she had ignored or insulted them.

Her whole world revolved around her son. He was her lover.

She was a pompous fool. A possessive mother. An intellectual with the brains of a monkey.

She slept with her son.

She was sleeping with her son!

There was a grain of truth here.

Even after Nanase came to work at the Shimizus, Shintaro would often sleep in Tsuneko's bedroom. Nanase had no idea what sweet nothings these two might have exchanged. But she did know that even when Shintaro slept alongside Sachie, they never talked like husband and wife. Nanase's room was directly across from their bedroom, so the couple's thoughts and feelings were constantly floating about her room. Even if Nanase didn't deliberately eavesdrop, any conversation they might have could not escape her notice.

As far as Nanase could tell, the couple didn't even have sexual relations. Judging by their mutual lack of interest, Nanase concluded that they had not touched each other for at least a year. Sachie had yet to experience an orgasm and didn't seem to care very much. She was still unable to think of herself as Shintaro's wife. She was painfully aware, however, that she was Tsuneko's daughter-in-law.

Things will get a bit easier for Sachie. Her three years of suffering are over.

So thought Sachie's father as he offered incense. But Nanase knew that Sachie's real troubles were just beginning. For now with his mother dead, Shintaro was emotionally stranded.

My son-in-law's an idiot. Sachie's two elder sisters are making a go of it. What a shame! That Sachie had to get stuck with this guy. Maybe he'll come to me for advice. I might be able to convince him to treat Sachie better.

Sachie's father didn't realize that Shintaro hated him even more than he himself hated Shintaro. He was the last person Shintaro would turn to for advice or support. From Shintaro's viewpoint, anyone who cared more for Sachie than for him was a natural enemy. With the hypersensitivity of a narcissist, Shintaro had intuited that everything Sachie's father had ever said to him originated from a fatherly concern for Sachie, and he took this as a personal offence.

You can't let down your guard with him. In a roundabout way, he's asking you to build a house. This show of concern is just a way for him to unleash his resentment. He claims that he's worried over your future, but his daughter is the only one he really cares about.

What he's saying is that he wants you to work harder for Sachie's sake.

Tsuneko had often spoken like this to Shintaro, making him distrust and resent his father-in-law.

She had taught Shintaro to disdain and make fun of everyone, not just relatives. Shintaro's condescending attitude, now second nature, was the product of Tsuneko's education. So Shintaro wasn't being paranoid when he felt that everyone around him was his enemy. He really was hated.

He's not stupid, but he's always fighting with his colleagues. I'm through looking after your son.

Shintaro's boss, head of the engineering department, spoke to Tsuneko in his mind while he offered incense. Shintaro's father had done him a favour once, so at Tsuneko's request he had recommended Shintaro for a position in his company and placed him in his own department. Shintaro's academic record was excellent, so he hadn't seen the harm in hiring him at the time. Now he wished he had paid more attention to the kind of person Shintaro was.

I made a mistake. What makes it my job to play up to your son? I'm sick of it and I'm sick of him. No more. I've had it. I've more than fulfilled my obligations. After your husband died, you were under the delusion that you wielded the same authority over people. What a pain in the neck you were. But I don't have to play up to your delusions any longer.

I'm through looking after your son.

He's twenty-seven — a grown man. I feel sorry for him, but...

His talent's going to waste, but... The score is even now.

Shintaro was about to be forsaken by the one person in the company who had looked out for him. Everyone else had given up on Shintaro a long time before. His selfishness and obstinacy were more than any normal person could put up with.

No one denied that Shintaro had a special talent for his job. But in a large company, efficient teamwork was more important than individual genius.

His skills are superb, and he's got the ability to develop new technology. But he's unable to compromise. If he can't get his own way, he throws a fit. He refuses to take orders. Sulks. Hates working with others. Makes fun of his co-workers. Starts his own projects without permission. Won't recognize anyone else's opinion. Gets into a huff. A loner. Hysterical. Vents his anger at everyone. Violent. Breaks things. Cries when reprimanded. Then runs home in tears. So he can tell Mummy. Afterwards she calls me at home late at night. Endless complaints.

But he can't run home to Mummy any more.

She'll never call me again. I've been too soft on them. Too soft on both mother and son. It's just him now.

I'm washing my hands of him.

There's nothing else I can do.

Nanase felt the department chief was perfectly justified in abandoning Shintaro. Trying to cater to Shintaro's whims had created even more problems with the other workers.

Nanase herself planned to leave when the funeral was over. She was curious to see what would happen to Shintaro, but most likely he would leave his job and then take out his frustrations on Sachie and even Nanase. She had no intention of babysitting a spoilt twenty-seven-year-old. In any case, Nanase had been hired to look after Tsuneko, and now that she was dead, there was no reason to stay.

He should fall as far as he can, thought Nanase. Once he hits rock bottom, he'll either pull himself together

207

or not, depending on his own efforts and how much Sachie helps him. Nanase felt sorry for Sachie, but her problems were no concern of hers.

In my situation, I can't afford to worry about anyone else, thought Nanase as she made her way to the altar. She was the last to offer incense. As Nanase predicted, the guests suddenly turned curious eyes towards her, and their various speculations and lewd fantasies came flooding into her mind.

Who is she? She's pretty. A real beauty.

Why is such a pretty girl working as a maid?

I wonder if she's a relative.

From among the minds of the many guests focusing their attention on her, Nanase suddenly picked up a bizarre thought that was so weak it seemed on the verge of fading away. Somebody was denouncing Sachie in their mind.

Sachie. I'll get you.

Nanase wondered who it was. She was surprised to find someone among the guests who hated Sachie that much. But in a matter of moments the weak signals were drowned out by the speculations going on inside the minds of all the other guests.

Twenty-two or twenty-three. No, probably younger.

She's so pretty and in her prime. Why does she wear her hair that way? It doesn't suit her at all.

With a figure like that she couldn't be a maid.

She must be a girl helping out from the neighbour-hood.

What proportions. Those hips. If she wore make-up, she'd be even...

The reaction was just as Nanase feared. Whether she wanted to or not, she had to recognize the incongruity between her childish hairstyle and her fully developed figure and good looks. What other girl would find her own body and pretty features such a burden or be afraid of men's admiring glances? She dashed off to the kitchen as soon as she finished offering incense.

Nanase was seriously considering looking for a new line of work. She was almost twenty years old. She would miss the safety of being a maid, flitting from one family to another, never staying long enough for anyone to guess her powers. She hadn't decided what she'd do next, but she would have to find a job where a pretty, unmarried girl wouldn't attract suspicion and where her secret could be easily kept.

Tsuneko's younger brother, Shigezo, came to the kitchen to talk to Nanase while she was putting away the dishes.

"Your name's Nana, isn't it?"

She looks much younger close up. What a waste for her to be a maid. Skin like rice cakes. If she'd use make-up, if she was wearing a nice dress...

Nanase's body tensed as she nodded.

The forty-eight-year-old Shigezo directed his youth-starved middle-aged gaze at Nanase's shapely breasts. "Do you plan to stay on here?"

I'll hire you. If we're living in the same house, at some point I'll have a chance. I'll buy you nice clothes.

"I guess you won't be needed here any more."

Sex. Young flesh. Sex.

Nanase nodded again.

"I've decided to quit being a maid." If I lived in his house, I wouldn't be able to sleep in peace, thought Nanase. She shuddered and dismissed him out of hand. But he didn't seem to think it odd that she was working as a maid, so Nanase relaxed her guard a bit.

"That's too bad." The disappointed Shigezo decided to get his fill of her while he had the chance and stared unreservedly at her behind.

What a nice behind. Damn. If she had worked at my house...

This was the first time someone had wanted to hire Nanase with an ulterior sexual motive. She was right after all in thinking that it was time to stop being a maid.

"What are you planning on doing?"

Shigezo still hadn't given up hope. He was thinking that even if she wasn't his maid, he could seduce her one way or another.

We'll be friends. Dates. An overnight trip. Jewellery.

Surprisingly enough, he even had confidence in his own looks. There was only one way left to discourage him.

"I'm getting married," Nanase said.

Shigezo's desires were instantly crushed. All at once he turned angry. His mind worked exactly like his sister Tsuneko's.

"Get me some tea," he said gruffly as he plopped himself down by the kitchen table. Meaningless sparks were flying inside his consciousness.

Flesh. Girls. My, my, my – sex. Hostesses. Nightclub hostesses. As much as you like. That kind of girl. Much better than her. Lots. Flesh. Flesh. Mymymy. My. Mine. Sex.

Fragments of feelings and bits of thoughts that even he couldn't understand came bursting out of his id. He took one gulp of the tea that Nanase handed him nervously and then noisily stood up.

"It's lukewarm." He glared at Nanase and stormed out.

The funeral service seemed to have ended. There was a stir in the living room.

Nanase was preparing tea for the priest when Sachie came into the kitchen and whispered into her ear. "Nana, would you mind driving with us to the crematorium? We can leave the cleaning up to the people from the funeral parlour."

Nanase quickly read Sachie's mind before agreeing. Shintaro had completely gone to pieces, and Sachie was afraid that she wouldn't be able to handle him alone.

They had already been carrying the coffin out of the house. Several men were trying to lower the coffin

211

from the veranda into the garden while Shintaro clung to it, sobbing. Some male relatives tried to pull him away, but Shintaro shook them off and held on even more furiously. His ego was in a state of semi-collapse. He was no different from a screaming infant. You could even say that he was experiencing a kind of orgasm. Some of the guests, who could no longer control their laughter, turned and broke into grins. One after another, people were covering their mouths with their handkerchiefs and giggling.

I've never been to such an interesting funeral.

It's like a comedy. If only I could take photographs.

Sachie, looking down in embarrassment, was walking next to the coffin, but as far away from her husband as possible. She had started hating Shintaro with a new-found intensity.

I have to consider it. Divorce. I have to consider it. I've nothing left to give him. What will Father say? I'll discuss it with him.

This might be for the best, thought Nanase. With Shintaro in his present condition, what good is there in trying to help him? What Shintaro needs now is to undergo all sorts of trials. If he can't bear up and goes crazy, then so be it. In Nanase's opinion, a Shintaro driven berserk by his mother's death would still be better off than a sane Shintaro unable to break away from his mother. At least he'd be one step closer to emotional independence.

Sachie. I'll get you.

Once more Nanase's antennae picked up this weak signal. Nanase spread out her feelers as she looked around her, but she couldn't find anyone who seemed to hate Sachie.

The coffin was placed inside the hearse. Eight limousines were on hand to take the relatives to the crematorium, but no one wanted to ride with Shintaro. Nanase and Sachie had to take charge of him, supporting the hysterical man on both sides.

Shintaro cried for almost the entire half-hour ride.

Inside the car, Nanase went over the faces of all the guests, and also searched Sachie's mind, looking for the person who was emitting those faint signals of anger. But she couldn't figure anything out.

She felt the signal for a third time when she stood in line with the relatives to watch the coffin go into the furnace. She stared terror-stricken at the coffin.

How could I not have noticed before, she chided herself. Shintaro's wailing was now even louder than ever, but she no longer heard it. All she could do was stare at the coffin, unable to move. She should have known right away that the consciousness was too weak to belong to a healthy person. No, even a sick person would have clearer thoughts than this. Was this the tenacious spirit of the dead then? Were these the remnants of a dying person's wrath left to float through the atmosphere? No, that wasn't it.

On the contrary, these thoughts, as intermittent as they were, seemed to be getting stronger and clearer all the time, gradually asserting their existence. Nanase stared, bewildered, at the sealed iron door of the furnace. In spite of the iron barrier, the thought patterns were more distinct than ever. It was a consciousness Nanase knew only too well. It was Tsuneko!

Had Tsuneko risen from the dead then? Had she come back to life inside the coffin? Was that possible? Nanase felt as if she had been hit over the head with a hammer. But even as she got over the shock, she was searching for some logical explanation for it all.

Sachie. Sachie's trying to kill me. She's plotting with the doctor. And the maid.

Shintaro. Shintaro. Open the lid. Get me out of here. I'm suffocating. It's dark.

Sachie. I'll get you.

The pain had turned Tsuneko's venom into a violent churning anger. The intensity of the thoughts emanating from the furnace was making Nanase shake in horror.

Nanase had read about incidents of premature burial. There was even a book claiming that people have little interest in the topic only because such cases are so rarely discovered, but in fact, resuscitation inside the coffin is far more common than anyone realized. The book showed how the posture of corpses dug up from graveyards proved that this horrible accident occurred one out of three times. Nanase had felt that instances of the dead coming back to life probably did happen before the advent of medical science, but they couldn't happen in this modern age where death can be precisely determined and cremation has become the norm.

Yet, in actuality, from inside her coffin, from inside the sealed furnace, Tsuneko was emanating a consciousness burning too strongly with anger and resentment to be considered that of the dead. And Nanase was the only one who knew that she had returned to life.

Only me.

Nanase flinched and, with head bowed, discreetly looked to her left and right. Neither the sobbing Shintaro nor the dozen relatives with their lowered heads had any inkling that Tsuneko had returned to life inside the soon-to-be-raging furnace. If Nanase didn't say anything, Tsuneko would be burnt alive without anyone ever realizing it.

If I don't say anything.

Nanase was in a quandary. A person's life or death depended on her. She wondered if deliberately shutting her eyes could be considered an act of murder. But how could she possibly tell them? Should she scream out, begging them to remove the coffin from the furnace? Should she tell them that Tsuneko had come back to life inside the coffin?

When she thought that far, Nanase was forced to shake her head weakly. No one would believe her, of course. She'd be dismissed as a sensitive young girl gone temporarily off the deep end.

Even if they did remove the coffin and rescue the fully conscious Tsuneko, how could Nanase explain how she knew that Tsuneko had returned to life? No half-baked explanation would suffice. The event would be so out of the ordinary that newspapers might get wind of it. In which case, some people might guess her power. In the worst scenario, it might become public knowledge. No, never, never, never, thought Nanase. She wrung her hands. For what purpose have I hidden my telepathic power up until now?

I don't know anything, I'm not telepathic, I can't hear anything, Nanase tried convincing herself. However, Tsuneko's screams and cries from her blazing hell-on-earth had turned into roaring shock waves that came surging non-stop into Nanase's mind.

It's hot. Hot. The smoke. My throat. Sachie. Sachie's killing me. I'm being murdered.

An image of Sachie's distorted face, looking like a demon, came to Nanase.

Sachie's plotted to have me killed.

Inside the fire, Tsuneko let loose her death cry. Consumed by the roaring inferno, her hair burst into writhing flames; she moaned like an animal facing death, paws clutching at air.

Help! Help! Shin... Shintaro. Shintaro. Shinta... Help! It's hot. Hot. Ohhhhhhhh...

Sachie. You've plotted with the maid. The maid...

When a deformed vision of Nanase's own face appeared in Tsuneko's thoughts, Nanase had to suppress

216

a scream. She tried closing her latch and shutting out Tsuneko's consciousness at the moment of death. But the frightening intensity of the dying woman's virulence would not let Nanase have her way. Defenceless, rooted to the spot, Nanase could only tremble in fear.

Because of the cremation, there'd be no proof that a body had regained life, so there were probably many instances of people cremated alive. This was just one example among many. Nanase kept making excuses to herself, but no matter what, she could not rid herself of the guilt she felt at so brazenly letting somebody die in order to protect herself. Nanase didn't believe in God, but she had learnt that she could not take the place of God.

Please forgive me. Die. Hurry up and die. Please die. You loved your son. As long as you're alive, your son will never amount to anything. Die for him. For your son's sake. Die for him.

Ohhhh. I'm dying. I'm dying. Dying.

I'm burning. Ashes. Ashes. Help. Help. I'm burning up. My whole body's in flames. Burning. Burn... Ohhhhhh...

Nanase clenched her teeth as these violent death cries reverberated inside her head. She joined her hands together in prayer, shut her eyes tightly and kept on chanting hoarsely.

Also by Yasutaka Tsutsui:

Salmonella Men on Planet Porno
ISBN 978 184688 077 3
£7.99

Defying the commonly held perceptions of
time and space, and escaping any easy clas-
sifications, this collection of stories centres
on the folly of human desire.

Hell
ISBN 978 184688 046 9
£7.99

This vivid depiction of afterlife includes the
traditional horrors, but subjects them to
Tsutsui's unique powers of enchantment.

Paprika
ISBN 978 184688 068 1
£9.99

Rich in humorous dialogue and ridiculous
situations, yet with an underlying sense of
menace, this literary sci-fi thriller has been
described as the pinnacle of Tsutsui's art.